The Young Rescuers

by

Donna B. Gawell

The Young Rescuers

Cover Art by *The Wild Rose Press, Inc.*

The Wild Rose Press, Inc.
PO Box 708
Adams Basin, NY 14410-0708
Visit us at www.thewildrosepress.com

Publishing History
First Edition, 2025
Trade Paperback ISBN 978-1-5092-6408-7
Digital ISBN 978-1-5092-6361-5

Published in the United States of America

Dedication

This novel is dedicated to my three grandchildren, Colin, Elise, and Naomi, the story's main characters. I hope they will be inspired by the true stories of real heroes woven into this story.

Introduction

The world needs to learn more about heroes who exemplify courage, the rarest of commendable human attributes. The Young Rescuers will introduce you to the stories of real people who risked their lives to rescue Jewish babies and children during the Holocaust.

The Young Rescuers is set in villages in occupied Poland near Camp Heidelager, the largest SS training camp outside Germany. The Germans invaded this region just days after declaring war on Poland on September 1, 1939. Camp Heidelager, located in the remote wilderness, was the perfect place for the Germans to conduct covert operations. Hitler referred to it as "Camp Wilderness."

Please realize that many characters and subplots were real as you read this book. Of course, fantasy and time travel offer an exciting approach to enhance the reading experience.

Only Irena Sendler's fellow rescuers from Warsaw and Sister Aniela are not actual historical people. Mishka's character is based on a well-known scoundrel from Kolbuszowa, an opportunistic traitor to the townspeople.

Monsignor Antoni Dunajecki recently received the prestigious designation "Righteous Among the Nations" from Yad Vashem, the World Holocaust Remembrance Center in Jerusalem, Israel. Donna Gawell considers her nomination of Monsignor Dunajecki as one of her most noteworthy accomplishments.

Readers can also learn more about Józef Bryk in the author's article written for The Doomed Soldiers Foundation, which is dedicated to the forgotten soldiers of Poland's Home Army 1944-1963. There is also information on him on DonnaGawell.com

Chapter One

The Gromnica Candle

Elise pointed to the mysterious golden candle sitting at the place of honor on the mantle in her grandparents' family room. "That's the magic candle, Naomi," Elise said, her voice tinged with both awe and caution. "Promise me, pinky swear to me, that you'll never lay a finger on it!"

Naomi's brown eyes sparkled with curiosity and playful defiance. "Why can't I?"

Elise propelled her fifteen-year-old petite body into a graceful aerial cartwheel, followed by a perfectly executed backflip, before offering an explanation for Naomi's innocent query. "All the grownups are worried about us using it to return to Poland. Mom's especially afraid Colin is going to light it again. She insisted that Grandma get it out of our house. That's why it's here at Grandma and Papa's house and not ours." Elise understood her parents' concerns all too well.

Naomi pushed a loose strand of her brown hair behind her ears. She stood utterly mesmerized in front of the lovely candle that had taken on mythical properties in her cousins' minds. "Don't you want to go back to Poland and help your relatives like you did last time, Elise?"

Elise stopped her gymnastics and surveyed the area

to be certain the cousins were alone. She checked to make sure the adults in the dining room wouldn't overhear their conversation. Satisfied with their privacy, she lowered her voice. "I'll admit, those months were the most exciting I'll probably ever have in my whole life, but Mom and Dad worry that something could go wrong if we go back."

"You got back safely. What possibly could go wrong if you went back again?" Naomi asked.

"Well, for one thing, it was during WWII. We were right there in probably the most dangerous area of Europe. But my parents' biggest worry is that Colin and I might be separated and wouldn't return together like we did last time." Elise shrugged her shoulders as she pondered that terrifying possibility. "I guess that could happen."

Both cousins stared at the glittering Gromnica candle with its blackened wick. It wasn't that Elise didn't want to return. Before the experience in Poland, she was a timid, slightly nervous little girl who found comfort in a doll or stuffed animal. During World War II, Elise had blossomed into a fearless young partisan because of her time travel adventures. Like Robin Hood, she stole food from the evil Germans to provide for the starving Polish partisans living in the forests. Within just a few months, Elise had acquired the stealthy skills of a spy, undertaking acts of espionage and rescue. When she returned home, Elise's more cautious nature seemed to have returned and tamed her wartime warrior spirit.

"I agree that the candle sure is pretty," Elise lamented. "But Grandma's cousin in Poland told her you're not supposed to light it unless there's a lightning storm or someone is dying." Elise's pensive, faraway look showed she had learned this caution was true. Lighting the candle had consequences she once would have never imagined.

"Eww. That sounds pretty scary!" Naomi grimaced. Then, her eyes were drawn to the bookcase. She rushed over to it and pulled out a children's book. "Look, Elise. Grandma read this to me last night. It's about a lady who saved thousands of Jewish babies during the war. Lots of Polish Girl Scouts helped rescue babies before the Germans could kill them. Maybe we could use the candle to go help this lady."

Elise smiled at her cousin's naïve enthusiasm. "Naomi, millions of people died in the war. We can't save all of them."

Naomi clutched the book to her chest and stood in a defiant posture. "Elise, I'm a Girl Scout and took their pledge. We're supposed to help others in need."

Elise tightened the tie on her ash-brown hair and collapsed on the couch in exasperation. "Naomi, it doesn't work like that. Colin and I didn't know we would become partisans in the Home Army when he first lit the Gromnica. Back then, we didn't know anything about the war except a few things Grandma told us about her relatives there."

"Don't you think we should at least try? If we went back in time, I would also be invisible to the Germans since we're cousins."

Elise sat cross-legged with her head resting on her hands. "Colin wants to go back in the worst way to help Uncle Józef." She tilted her head to see if any adults were nearby. Then she whispered, "Don't tell my parents, but Colin's been researching the time after the war when those evil Russians took over Poland. Polish partisans like Uncle Józef were considered the enemies of the Russians. The Russians arrested and then killed Polish soldiers. He's found hardly anything helpful on the internet because most of it is written in Polish. Not like all the stuff on that V-2 missile, Hitler's top secret weapon. There are tons of stuff in English about that."

Naomi's face lit up with excitement. "You mean Colin wants to go back?"

"Oh, yeah. Really bad, and Colin says he'll do it even if he has to wait until he's all grown up." Elise's demeanor remained serious. "Colin knows our parents would never agree to let him go even if his intentions are honorable."

A wide smile spread across Naomi's face at the thought of an adventure with her six-foot-tall cousin with tousled chestnut hair. She had always adored him. At age seventeen, Colin gave the impression he was too cool to hang around an eleven-year-old. His aloof manner was no match for the strong-willed Naomi. "I'm going to ask Colin if I can go with him. We'd be such a great team!" She then noted Elise's dismissive smirk and raised eyebrows. "Don't worry. I'll wait to ask him when we're all in the tent so our parents can't hear us."

"Oh, Naomi!" Elise sighed, realizing her confidence-filled cousin would not be deterred. "Maybe after you graduate from college."

****

The nighttime belonged to the crickets and tree frogs singing from the ravine behind the grandparents' house. The three cousins smoothed out their sleeping bags and settled in for the night in the tent. Engrossed in a game on his tablet, Colin was abruptly interrupted by a hurried crackling. He flashed the light from his cell phone onto his dogs, Noah and Leia. "Dang, Noah got into the snack bag already." Colin whisked the friendly Great Pyrenees away from the bag of cookies and stuffed them under his pillow.

"Naughty dog!" Naomi bounced up and down on her knees as she hugged Noah. The novelty of hanging out with her cousins' dogs was exhilarating. "That was a funny story about how Noah stole a sausage from the Nazis on your last adventure, and all they could see was the sausage flying in the air because Noah was invisible to the Germans. I guess dogs in the family are somehow included in that invisibility thing."

"I wanted to strangle Noah when he did that!" Elise said. "I thought for sure the Germans saw me waiting for him at the edge of the forest. I would have been a goner if they had seen me."

Naomi leap-frogged in front of her cousin with a huge grin on her face. "Colin, I'm going with you next time you travel to Poland. I want to help rescue the Jewish babies so they don't die."

"You're not going with me!" Colin sneered at Naomi's suggestion and defiantly crossed his arms. "I'm going alone when the time is right. Maybe I'll take Noah, but I'm flying solo next time." Colin coaxed the Great Pyrenees to lie next to him. "Even if he is a big pig."

Naomi harrumphed and folded her arms to mimic Colin. "Hey, Colin. Do you have a lady friend yet?"

"None of your business, Naomi." Colin rolled over to face the tent wall and resumed his solitary video game. "Ugh. How did I ever let Grandma talk me into sleeping in this tent with you guys?"

Elise kneeled next to Leia, petting the pudgy little Corgi. "Grandma says the dogs can't stay in the tent all night, so maybe they should go inside now."

"I'll go with you!" Naomi sprang to her feet to join her cousin and the dogs. "We'll be right back, Colin."

Colin zipped open the tent door for the girls and smirked. "Watch out for the coyotes."

Naomi froze but then realized Colin was teasing. "There aren't any coyotes around here, Mr. Smarty-pants." Naomi ran with Noah to the back door and hurried inside.

Colin mumbled as he zipped up the tent door. "Like I'd ever take an eleven-year-old back to Poland during World War II."

Minutes later, Elise scurried back into the tent.

"Where's Naomi?" Colin asked.

"Don't know, but it sure is taking Naomi a long time to use the bathroom. Maybe she's scared and decided to sleep in her bed instead of out here," suggested Elise.

"Doubt it. Naomi's pretty fearless. Maybe she just went to call her parents again."

The screen door squeaked open and then clanked shut. Colin sat up, peered out the tent's side window, and spotted Naomi approaching her tent. "She's baackkk!" Colin moaned.

Naomi clumped down the deck stairs, zipped open the tent door, and crawled inside with her backpack.

"Why'd you bring your backpack out here, Naomi?" Elise asked. "We're not going on a hike."

"This is my Girl Scout backpack. It has my flashlight, guidebook, and compass. Everything I'll need." Naomi unzipped her pack to display her treasures.

Elise smiled at her young cousin's enthusiasm, but had lots of experience with Naomi's hyperness. "If you'll lie down now and try to rest, I'll tell you one of the fairytales Maria taught me." Elise looked up and drummed her fingers over her lips as if trying to search her memory. "Which one do you want to hear? The one about the bear in the forest hut or one called Prince Kindhearted?"

Colin rolled onto his stomach and pretended to cover his ears. "Hey, you two. We have to get up early for my lacrosse game tomorrow, and Naomi, you won't need your little Girl Scout supplies tonight."

A slight click followed by a faint flicker of light swallowed up the blackness inside the tent. Colin growled, "Naomi, turn off your flashlight and go to sleep!"

"It isn't a flashlight!" Elise screamed. "Naomi! Blow that candle out now before the whole tent catches on…!"

Colin shot up from his sleeping bag but only saw darkness inside the tent. "Naomi, you didn't light the gromnica, did you?" He flashed the light from his cell phone onto Naomi, holding only a butane lighter, but no gromnica was in view. "Good thing Elise blew it out!"

"Colin, I saw the gromnica candle in Naomi's hand just a few seconds ago, but now it's not here anymore," Elise said.

"Give me that lighter, Naomi!" Colin yelled. "What did you just do?"

An ominous sense of the unreal surrounded the tent. At first, it sounded like a large branch from a nearby tree had cracked and fallen to the ground in a thunderous crash. The children's bodies stiffened, and they cautiously glanced around the tent. Then, an unearthly howl squealed and wailed as it circled the tent, but what on earth was it? It matched nothing in the catalog of plausible things it might be at this time of night. Not a pack of coyotes or other wild animals ascending from the ravine. Not a police helicopter that sometimes would swoop through the woods searching for some illegal activity.

"I've never heard anything like this before except maybe in sci-fi." Colin crawled on his knees to look out the tent window but saw only darkness. "I'm going to call Grandma and Grandpa to come to the back door in case there's a coyote near the tent." He tapped his grandfather's number, but the phone just kept on ringing. "I'll try Grandma's to see if hers is working."

Elise crawled up to the window and lifted the flap. "Colin! Look! We're not in Grandma's backyard!"

Colin leaped to the tent door and pushed open the flap to notice the sun peeking over the horizon. An old wooden house stood in the distance with a fence all around it. He recognized the landscape as somewhat familiar but was certain they were no longer in America. "Are we back in Poland? I can barely make out that old house over there. It looks like the kind they had in Poland a long time ago, but that isn't Jadwiga's house."

Elise shuddered when she also realized that a new adventure was possibly in front of them. "Colin, I think it is World War II Poland, but I don't recognize any of this."

Chapter Two

Grandpa Andrzej

The ancient Sandomierz forest reeked of age. Its woody fragrance, earned from centuries of once-mighty oaks and pine trees, rose up as the children emerged from the protection of their tent. The trees started to shiver, and what seemed like a barn owl swooped down onto the moist woodland floor.

"Let's go check out that old house down that path," Colin said. He and Elise walked on the trail flanked by prickly brambles and berry bushes leading to the cottage. Twigs and dead leaves made a deafening crunch under their feet, and the smell of burning wood billowed through the early morning air.

Elise and Colin turned to find Naomi trailing behind. Her lips trembled, and her dark lashes brimmed heavy with tears. Then the floodgates opened, and heaving sobs tore through her throat. She choked through her crying. "I'm sorry! I'm so, so sorry!"

"You've got to be quiet, Naomi." Colin blew out a distressed, heavy breath, uncertain of his next step.

"Listen, a dog is barking, but it sounds like it's coming from that house," Elise said.

"Elise, look! An old lady is coming out of that house, and she's coming this way, sort of." Colin squinted and saw the woman's quivering hands frantically tapping at her cheeks. "Now she's rushing back into the house."

Colin cautioned the girls to stop. "She must have seen us."

"She sure looks nervous, like an alien spaceship just landed in her yard," Elise said. "I guess our tent sort of looks like one."

In less than a minute, an older man stepped outside the house. He hoisted up his pants and stretched his suspenders over his shoulders. He stood at a distance, holding an oil lantern in one hand while stroking his graying mustache with the other.

"Colin, I think that's Grandpa Andrzej! Look at his bushy mustache. I'm sure of it!"

"Naomi, don't worry. I think that man is our great-great-great-grandfather. We met him before! Everything will be okay!" Colin hugged his sobbing cousin. "You stay here."

Colin and Elise shouted out as they approached him. "Grandpa Andrzej!"

The old man froze and stumbled backward, almost falling into his rhubarb patch. His eyes darted between the two children, but he stood staring in disbelief.

"Grandpa Andrzej, do you remember us, your great-grandchildren from America? Our grandmother is your daughter Marya's granddaughter!" Colin said. "From Cleveland."

"Family from America?" Andrzej uttered, but his words dripped with doubt and unbelief. How could his family from the United States just show up on his farm? And in wartime?

"Yes, we were here before, in 1944, right before the war ended. We met you and Father Kurek and Lord

Hupka," Colin offered.

"And our other grandmother, Jadwiga, and her son Józef and Maria, too!" Elise explained.

"But it's 1942, not 1944. How can this be?" Andrzej stood frozen while he pondered the mysterious scene in his midst. "Who's the little one peeking out from behind the shed?"

Colin signaled for Naomi to join them. "Naomi, this is your great-grandfather Andrzej. Remember, we told you all about him."

Andrzej had no idea what was happening, but the sight of a frightened child warmed his heart. "Oh, little Naomi is afraid. Come closer, little one."

Naomi shuffled over but stood behind her older cousins until they heard a voice pierce the still morning air.

"Andrzej, bring those refugee children in for something to eat. They must be hungry!"

"They're not refugees, Zeffie. They're our grandchildren from America, I think." Andrzej responded.

"Children, do you also remember your Grandma Zeffie?" Andrzej asked.

All three shook their heads. Elise quickly chimed in, "No, I don't remember her at all, but we never visited your house before. Maybe that's why we don't recognize her." Colin looked at his sister with grateful eyes. Only he and Elise knew that Zeffie would soon have a stroke and die in 1943.

"Come inside and explain this mystery to me," Andrzej exclaimed. "You children from America dress much differently than the clothes I've seen in the photographs from Michal and my Marya."

Elise whispered to Colin, "Here we go again, trying to explain who we are and how we can travel through time."

Chapter Three

The Baby

Shadows danced upon the lime-washed walls illuminated by oil lamps and candles as Elise and Naomi sat silently in Andrzej and Zeffie's small cottage. Naomi was mesmerized by her ancestors' small, shabby home. Her eyes flitted around the room to examine each household item. She shivered as she studied the dower religious paintings on the walls. The religious people in the pictures seemed to stare down at her with disapproval. Naomi then remembered Elise had described these scary images.

Elise couldn't help but notice the striking resemblance between the Cudecki house and the homes of her other ancestors she had seen during her first visit. The heart of the house was the massive clay oven, where heavy black pots and kettles hung from hooks. The large wooden table, worn smooth by generations of family meals, stood at the center of the room. Elise recalled how the family had spent most of their time in this very space, sharing stories and laughter around the oven and table. The only haven of comfort in the home was the bed, with its soft, plush blankets. Despite its sometimes scratchy straw-stuffed mattress, the bed was always a serene retreat after a strenuous day of hard work.

Colin sat at the table with Andrzej and Zeffie, attempting to explain how they could time travel because of a gromnica.

Andrzej rested his chin on his folded hands, his eyes wide in amazement. "So, you're telling me that we can see and hear you, but you're invisible to anyone who isn't your relative?"

Colin shrugged his shoulders. "I know it sounds peculiar, but that's the way it worked last time. I sure hope it's the same this time, too."

Zeffie's nerves began to ease, but then she observed how uncomfortable Elise and Naomi appeared. She squeezed in between the two girls, who had found a seat on the bench with Colin. She took turns stroking and caressing their innocent faces with her aged, arthritic hands. "I'm so blessed! How many old people can say they've met their great-great-great-grandchildren?" Zeffie stroked each girl's curls and kept shaking her head in amazement. "You really are human children! God has blessed us with a miracle!"

Colin wasn't sure how much he should explain about their last trip with Zeffie sitting there. Zeffie seemed a nervous sort of woman, and he didn't want to cause her more worry.

Andrzej stroked his moustache. "So, only your blood relatives can see you, but the Germans can't?"

"We tested it out last time with the Polish partisans in the forests. The ones related to us could see us, but the others couldn't. None of the Nazis ever noticed us." Colin said.

"Partisans in the forest? In our forests?" Zeffie's voice trembled as she burst into another fit of anxiety. "There are only Jewish refugees who escaped the camps or ghettos. Maybe a few of our soldiers who escaped from the prison, but there is no army in our forests."

Both Colin and Elise had learned a lot about Poland since their last adventure. They didn't know how to answer Zeffie's concerns accurately. "I remember Alex telling me that it took a few years for the young Polish soldiers to reorganize after Hitler invaded in 1939. Pretty soon, there will be lots of partisan soldiers fighting for Poland's freedom," Colin said. "They're fighting for everyone who lives here."

"The big question is when will the war end?" asked Andrzej. "You must know that answer."

"Sort of, but it seems that some things Elise and I did helped save some people, which then changed history. So, I'm not totally sure my answer is correct, but it seems you were liberated in 1944. It took longer in other places in Europe," Colin replied.

Zeffie's eyes lit up. "Was it the Americans who saved us? Jadwiga, your other grandmother, and I are certain our American grandsons will come looking for us! They're sailors and soldiers, you know."

"I'm pretty sure you must mean my great-grandfather Stanley. He was in other parts of Europe. But yes, the Allies helped drive the Nazis out of Niwiska sometime around August 1944."

Andrzej stood and shook his head as he shuffled to the stove for another cup of coffee. "Two more years? Two more years of living under the Germans?"

A wailing noise burst from the other room, and Zeffie jumped up and ran to respond.

"What was that? It sounds like a baby!" Elise exclaimed.

Zeffie emerged from the doorway with a baby in her arms. She cradled it as if the child were the most fragile treasure in the world. Her work-worn hands, knotted slightly with age, held the small bundle with practiced care. The infant's tiny fingers clutched at the edge of the woolen shawl wrapped snugly around it. The two girls sprinted to get a peek at the baby and cooed with excitement.

Andrzej leaned forward and stroked his brow. "Children, we're happy to meet you, but, as you can see, you couldn't have arrived at a worse time."

Colin seemed to be the only one who took notice of Andrzej's ominous words. "Why is this the worst time for us to come? What's going on?"

"Two days ago, the Germans announced that almost everyone in this region will be evacuated by the weekend. We'll all have to leave our homes and find a place to live outside of Camp Heidelager."

Elise twirled around, and she stared intently at Andrzej. "You have to leave?" She then remembered hearing stories from her uncle Józef. He had told her the Germans destroyed most of the homes in Niwiska to expand Camp Heidelager, the largest SS training camp outside of Germany. Realizing it was best not to reveal what she knew of their future, Elise walked over to Andrzej and put her arm around him. "Whatever happens, you'll be back here way before July 1944 because that's when we first met you."

"Thank you for comforting this old man, my darling Elise. But what will happen to all my family, my children, and my grandchildren? And, especially this new little one?" Andrzej pointed to the infant, now cradled in Naomi's eager arms.

"Grandpa Andrzej, is this your grandchild? What's its name? Is it a boy or a girl? I can't tell." Naomi whispered in low tones, holding the baby's head stiffly.

"Babies all look the same until you change their diapers."

Zeffie stroked the baby's dark curls. "He's a boy. We call him Pawel." Andrzej and Zeffie sat silently and then gazed at one another. "Should they be told, Andrzej?"

Andrzej nodded and breathed a heavy sigh. "I'm going to tell you children something, but it must be a secret to everyone because our lives depend on no one else knowing. He's been with us for a week. No one, not even our neighbors, must know he's here. Especially the Germans."

Zeffie tapped her gnarled fingers together nervously. "When neighbors hear him cry, we tell them we are keeping our daughter's baby while they search for a place to live. But we can't keep him after we move."

Colin and Elise's eyes looked down, knowing that Andrzej must have good reasons. They had learned some of the hard lessons of war during their first adventure.

"Why? Why can't you keep him?" Naomi blurted. "Just take him with you!"

Zeffie put her arm around Naomi. "Dear one, you know nothing about how the Germans hate the Jews. They would kill this child if they found him here...and they would kill everyone in this house also."

Colin understood his cousin's ignorance. He previously had known next to nothing about World War II or the Holocaust. That first experience forced him to grow up quickly and understand the complex realities of war. "Naomi, what Andrzej and Zeffie are trying to tell us is that this baby is a Jew. The Germans want all Jews to be killed, every single one of them. Even a baby."

Their relatives had also told Elise about how brutally the Germans treated Jews during the war. "It's

17

against the law to even give food or water to a Jew. If the Germans found Andrzej and Zeffie with this baby, well, that would be the end of the family and anyone who happened to be around."

Colin looked away as he tried to contain his hatred of the occupiers. "The Germans don't ask questions. They just shoot."

None of this made complete sense to Naomi. "But, why can't you take him with you to your new home?"

Andrzej understood Naomi's confusion. "Look closely. He has dark hair, olive skin, and dark eyes. The Germans would know he was Jewish, especially if they insisted on seeing if he was circumcised. Catholic Poles don't circumcise their sons, but Jewish parents do." Everyone could tell Naomi was still somewhat confused.

Zeffie interjected, "We need to place this baby with another family, but we have no time. We must begin leaving tomorrow." Her hands trembled as she reached for her apron to dab the tears welling up in her eyes. "Anyway, no one around here is in a position to take him. They're like us and need to evacuate."

Elise glanced at Colin and whispered, "Maybe this is why the gromnica sent us back to Niwiska...to this time and place. Maybe someone was going to die if we didn't light the gromnica?"

"Maybe this Jewish baby was going to die if we didn't time travel back to WWII?" Colin nodded and began to think like the young partisan he had been in 1944. "Can the three of us take Baby Pawel to Father Kurek to see if he can help?"

"You know our priest?" Andrzej asked in amazement.

Elise wished she could tell Andrzej and Zeffie how

they helped to save Father Kurek from the Germans who wanted to arrest him, but this wasn't the time.

"No, Father Kurek also has to evacuate and will be staying with Monsignor Dunajecki in Kolbuszowa," Zeffie said. "Priests could never take in a baby."

Andrzej methodically stroked his mustache as he considered Colin's suggestion. "No, Zeffie. They have a good idea. Father Kurek's still at the church in Niwiska preparing to evacuate," Andrzej said. "Our priest can't take the baby, but he may be able to find a family to take Pawel."

Elise beamed. "Then, that's where the three of us will go. We'll talk to Father Kurek and then come back for the baby before you leave."

Colin wasn't sure how to get to the church, but he had his cell phone for directions. "Don't worry. We know how to get to the church to find Father Kurek. We'll be safe."

"Don't worry about the three of us! We'll be safe because we're INVISIBLE!" Naomi exclaimed as she bounced up and down. "This is so cool!"

Chapter Four

Meeting Monsignor Dunajecki

Early the next day, the gray horse's hooves clip-clopped down the dry dirt road. Father Kurek held onto the reins as he and the children headed from Niwiska toward Kolbuszowa. "It's sad you didn't get to spend more time with Andrzej and Zeffie. They're fine Christian people." The young, smooth-faced priest with his bent, wire-framed spectacles was just as kind and pleasant as Elise and Colin remembered.

"We understand, though. It isn't safe for us to travel with Andrzej and Zeffie to a whole new town, especially since they don't even know exactly where they're going," said Colin. He and Elise knew their future, the story of how Andrzej and Zeffie traveled to a village called Radomysl, where they found a home abandoned by Jews. Their daughter and her family would also live there.

"I feel sorry for Zeffie, knowing she won't do well there," Elise said.

"Won't do well there? What do you mean by that, Elise?" Father Kurek asked.

"She's going to have a stroke and will be buried in a town that ends in Wilki," she replied.

"Radomysl Wilki?"

"Yeah, I think that's what it's called. Andrzej will

have to bury her there, but he'll come back here to live with his son."

Father Kurek raised his eyebrows and blew out a deep breath. "I forgot. You know some of our futures. It's probably best for us not to know our destinies." The priest was careful not to ask any more questions. "We need to get to town before curfew, so I'm going to push old Wojciech to get us there faster."

The priest jolted the reins of the Monsignor's horse to pick up the pace as they traveled on the back streets. With the heavy presence of Germans all around, he was always careful to take less-traveled routes.

Elise turned to see Naomi kissing the baby's forehead. "How are you doing back there with Baby Pawel, Naomi?"

Naomi just smiled and put her finger to her lips so the baby wouldn't awaken.

"We're entering Kolbuszowa now, children. Hide." Colin and Elise dove into the cart with Naomi, buried themselves below the hay, and remained perfectly still. Once at the rectory, Father Kurek hurried the children into the priests' residence's rear door.

"That had to be my scariest trip through Kolbuszowa since the beginning of the war," Father Kurek muttered under his breath.

Naomi transferred baby Pawel to Elise while Colin and Father Kurek carried their tent and supplies into the house. They wondered how all the items would be used in the future. Colin smiled when he noted a bag of tortilla chips was still in the tent.

"You three stay in the entryway while I find the monsignor." Father Kurek insisted and then reemerged just a few minutes later.

An older priest entered the foyer, and Father Kurek warmly greeted him. "In front of you are three real children, Monsignor." Father Jan Kurek's voice rose slightly as he excitedly explained the situation. "They can hear and understand you, but you can't see or hear them. I'll take you by the hand so you can touch the top of their heads."

"Is this some sort of a joke, Jan?" The tall, stately Monsignor Dunajecki stood in disbelief as he placed his hand on Colin's six-foot frame. "This is the boy? Lord, Jesus, this is no joke! He's almost my height." The priest then put his hands on Colin's shoulders. "Strong, too. He must like sports."

Colin smirked, "He guessed that right. I play hockey and lacrosse, but I've played almost every sport."

"Not gymnastics, I bet! That's what I do best," Naomi exclaimed as she began to show off with her best cartwheel.

"Not now, Naomi! We're in the priest's house." Elise said. "Good thing the monsignor didn't see that!"

"This is Naomi, whom I have just met. She is Colin and Elise's cousin from America," explained Father Kurek.

"How old is this child? She seems the size of our children who make their First Communion," said the monsignor as he stroked her hair.

Father Kurek signaled for Elise to come forward. "And this is our darling Elise. She has a beautiful voice and dances so well. I wish you could hear her sing."

Elise sweetly smiled and blushed as she lifted her eyebrows. "Tell Monsignor Dunajecki that we are pleased to meet him and that Naomi also dances and sings very well. We are cousins, after all."

Father Kurek shared more about the children and the story they had just communicated to him. "To be honest, Monsignor, I am just learning the story for the first time. They are also telling me about the future." The young priest took the girls by the hand to sit them on the formal parlor's red velvet sofa. "The more I talk with them, the more familiar they seem to me. I believe they are angels from the future in the form of children."

"And why is it that you can see and hear them, but I can't?" Dunajecki asked.

"I'm related to the Bryk family, and, therefore, we share enough blood for me to be amongst the privileged who can see them," Kurek explained.

The monsignor smiled, "So, they can see and hear me, but are invisible to the Germans."

Colin sat in the middle of the girls. "Father Kurek, maybe you should explain why we are here."

"Yes. Oh, right." Father Kurek began to stumble with his words. "Monsignor, their grandfather, Andrzej Cudecki, took in a Jewish baby from the forest a week ago. He and his wife need to place the baby in a safe home. Like most of the villagers in Niwiska and Trzesn, they are leaving very soon. He has nowhere else to turn."

"So, his request has to do with these three invisible children helping in some manner? The Germans wouldn't see them, but they would see the baby?"

"That's part of the wonderful mystery of these children. Everything they brought from the future, their blankets, clothes, and tents, can't be seen. Elise reminded me of when she and her huge dog Noah stole mounds of food from the Germans' storehouse. They used backpacks made out of her invisible blanket."

Dunajecki leaned back in his chair with his eyes

lifted to the ceiling. "Let me imagine a possibility." His eyes shifted back and forth, and then he nodded his head. "Perhaps Sister Roberta at the convent in Trzesowka will help us, but we need to plan this carefully. We'll all go to the Cudeckis' house this afternoon and transfer the baby in my wagon."

The children beamed, and Naomi jumped up and down. "This is the greatest day in my whole life!"

Father Kurek grinned. "Well, let's hope the nuns don't faint when they find out a Jewish baby has arrived with three invisible children. They may think you're all from outer space!"

Chapter Five

The Baby Arrives at the Convent

The children cowered under the bristling hay as
Father Kurek guided the weather-beaten cart down the
path to the convent. Colin peeked out to see where they
were. He tapped Naomi, "There's a sign in front of that
building. It says something like 'The Sisters of St.
Joseph.' See the name, Józef? That's how you spell
Joseph in Polish."

"Shh! Pawel is still sleeping." Naomi glared at her
older cousin, enjoying the opportunity to reprimand him.

Monsignor Dunajecki lowered himself off the seat
and rang the bell. A wooden window in the door slid
open, and the face of a nun appeared. Stiff white bands
covered her forehead and most of her chin. "Monsignor
Dunajecki! We didn't know you were coming."

Sister Barbara quickly unlocked the gate for the
monsignor. The younger priest guided the cart to the rear
of the convent. Once safely inside, he put his finger up
for the children to keep silent. After checking to see if
anyone witnessed their guests, the nun followed behind
until they arrived at the convent door.

Sister Barbara's sweet face and bright blue eyes
contrasted with the stiff veiling of her order. "Come!
Come inside. You haven't met the other sisters from
L'viv."

"I heard about how their convent was burned to the ground. So glad they escaped from the Ukrainians. They can be just as bad as the Germans," Father Kurek said.

Sister Roberta appeared and greeted the Monsignor and the priest. She was a tall, slender woman whose dark eyes held both intelligence and compassion. Her kind smile, framed by the starched edges of her habit, carried a serenity that seemed to soften the room.

"We weren't expecting you. Is there trouble in Kolbuszowa?"

Dunajecki lowered his voice and whispered, "Sister, I need to speak to you and the Mother Superior alone. None of the other sisters must see or hear us."

"Our Mother Superior is visiting convents in other areas. She is hoping to find a safer place for our sisters from Ukraine. I'm the sister responsible for the convent in her absence." Sister Roberta glanced quizzically at the mysterious cart. She then instructed the other sisters to wait inside the house and prepare a meal for the priests.

Once assured no one could see or overhear them, the monsignor signaled Sister Roberta to come near the cart. "What I am going to reveal to you is quite miraculous. In this cart are three children from the future. They are grandchildren of the Bryk and Cudecki families from the villages. You and I can't see them, but I assure you they're quite real."

Father Kurek interjected, "I'm able to see and hear them only because we are related, so I'll help you all to communicate with them."

Colin and Elise popped their heads from beneath the hay while Naomi slowly emerged with a baby in her arms. To Dunajecki and the nun, it appeared the babe was floating in midair.

Sister Roberta clutched her crucifix. "Holy Jesus, what am I seeing here?"

"Naomi, the youngest child, is holding a Jewish baby who needs to be hidden."

"A Jewish baby?" Sister Roberta stammered as she put her hand to her chest. "Of course, Monsignor, of course."

"His Polish name will be Pawel. His father brought him to the Cudeckis from the ghetto and promised to pay for his care. He gave Andrzej these gold coins." The priest then transferred the money to Sister Roberta.

"So, are his parents amongst the Jews being taken to the detention camp in Rzeszów?"

"Yes, sadly, that is their fate. That place is sure death for every Jew sent there." The Monsignor made the sign of the cross. "Some Jews have paid a huge ransom for a group of Jews to be returned to Kolbuszowa, but their efforts are futile. No one who goes to that detention camp is ever heard from again."

"Monsignor, the hay is moving!" exclaimed the nun. "Are the other children in this wagon? Before my very eyes?"

"The Monsignor and I think of them as angels sent from God above," Father Kurek said.

"Bring the children into the convent for some soup." Sister Roberta scurried to the convent door but then hesitated. "Or, don't they eat since they are invisible?"

Father Kurek laughed loudly. "They certainly do, especially the boy who's almost as tall as the Monsignor."

Naomi skipped to the convent door. "Soup! I love soup!"

"That's good because pretty much that's what you'll

be eating morning, noon, and night. Soup." Elise smiled, remembering how she hated soup when she was younger. After living with the Bryks during those months, she learned to appreciate more humble foods. "Don't be like I was at first. Dumb me asked for chicken nuggets."

"Don't they have chicken nuggets?" Naomi asked.

Elise sighed, "Naomi. There are no freezers or even refrigerators around here. This is Poland during the Second World War."

In the small dining hall, Sister Roberta poured the sour rye soup over a few pieces of hard-to-secure sausage and bread cubes into the brown clay bowls. Elise and Colin recognized it as a soup their grandmother called zurek, made from rye wheat.

Monsignor Dunajecki's eyes lit up. "Sister, you are too generous. You mustn't give us this precious meat from your limited reserves."

The nun chuckled, "How often does a person get to feed angels and the priests who brought them to her home?"

"Father Kurek, would you ask Sister Roberta if we can come back to visit Pawel?" Naomi asked.

"I doubt it, but don't worry about him. Pawel will have lots of women to play and care for him at the convent. It is more important that we all help them keep Pawel a secret." The young priest stroked Naomi's shiny brown hair. "Think of how you just helped here. You three brought the baby here safely. The Monsignor and I could have never done that by ourselves."

Sister Aniela, one of the youngest nuns, nudged the door open with her elbow, balancing a stack of plates in her hands. "Children! I had no idea we were expecting children at the convent!"

Everyone froze in place. Sister Roberta shot a frantic look at Father Dunajecki. If Sister Aniela could see the three children, the cousins possibly wouldn't be as safe as they first thought. In a calm voice, she said, "Tell me who you see at the table, Sister Aniela. In detail."

"Tell you who I see?" Bewildered, the young nun obediently pointed to each person as she spoke. "There is the Monsignor at the head of the table. Father Kurek is on one side of the table with a young, brown-haired girl next to him. Across from them is a tall boy with straight blond hair and a girl younger than the boy to his left. Their clothing is like nothing I have ever seen. So bright and colorful."

"Ask them some questions to see what else you can learn about them," the Monsignor insisted.

The young nun began to tremble, realizing something was very wrong. Children didn't just show up at the convent like this. "They can't be Jews because they look like Poles." She looked at Elise. "All right. Tell me where you are from and recite the Lord's Prayer."

Elise stood and pushed back her wavy, light brown hair. "I'm from Niwiska, right now anyway." She then recited the prayer to perfection.

"You added some extra words at the end, but that was very natural and quite perfect and beautiful," said the young nun. "I grew up in nearby Kolbuszowa and have never seen you before." Sister Aniela approached the children to get a closer look. "Where did you get these peculiar clothes from?"

Father Kurek looked quizically at the nun. "Sister Aniela, tell us the names of your grandparents and great-grandparents," said Father Kurek.

"Bryk, Lakomy, Koch. Those are the ones I remember," answered the younger nun.

"Ah, Bryk, Lakomy! So, Sister Aniela is related to these young people, just like me." Everyone let out a collective sigh of relief. "Who are your parents?" asked Father Kurek.

"Adam and Cunegunda Koch. They died when my brother and I were young children. My brother and I are all that remain," she answered.

"Sister Aniela, you are not to tell the others about these children. They are under the Monsignor's protection. Do you understand what I am saying?" Sister Roberta's firm command left no doubt about the seriousness of the situation.

Monsignor Dunajecki stood next to Sister Aniela. "I assure you, they are not Jews, so you don't have to worry about any danger."

Sister Aniela's eyes widened, and her head bobbed rapidly in agreement as the monsignor towered over her. Then, Sister Roberta signaled for her to leave the room.

"We never had that happen before," said Colin. "I guess it was because we met with so few people outside of our family."

"Don't worry, children. Sister Aniela is related to you through the Koch family, but we don't want any more surprises like that. Especially if it is someone who might want to tell others," Father Kurek said.

"Monsignor, the children might be safer here, away from Kolbuszowa. There could be many of their possible relatives walking around." Sister Roberta clutched her hands confidently. "Eventually, I'll bring Sister Aniela into our confidence. She can assist us in communicating with the children."

"How do you feel about that, children?" Monsignor Dunajecki asked.

"I do feel safer here. Kolbuszowa has so many Germans and trucks." Elise's eyebrows raised, and her eyes began to tear. "All the shouting and trucks in town make me so nervous."

"I guess it would be less boring here." Colin shook his head to agree. "Maybe we could help with the farm animals, although we don't really know anything about taking care of animals."

"Except for dogs," Elise blurted.

Naomi defiantly folded her arms. "How about me?"

"Of course. What are your thoughts, Naomi?" Father Kurek asked.

Naomi grinned widely and jumped up and down like she was wound with a spring. "Now that we're living here, I get to take care of Baby Pawel!"

Everyone smiled at Naomi's innocent optimism.

"Time to find you three more suitable clothing. We need to make you look like Polish children," Monsignor Dunajecki laughed. "Off I go to town to see what I can find on the black market!"

Chapter Six

Meeting Anna Grabiec

Anna, a serious young woman, had the steady composure of someone who had endured three long years of war in Poland. Her dark brown hair was drawn neatly back, framing a face marked more by quiet determination than youth's carefree glow. She wiped the perspiration from her brow. Swinging her leg over the bicycle frame, she dismounted and approached the convent gate, the dust of the road clinging to her skirt. Her fingers lingered for a moment on the brass bell, and a brief prayer passed through her mind before she rang it. A moment later, Sister Aniela opened the wooden window, her face brightening at the sight of her childhood friend. "Anna, come in. The Monsignor is already here."

"How are you, Sister Aniela?"

Sister Aniela looked over her shoulder to see if any of the others were nearby. "Something strange is going on here, Anna. I fear that the Germans might make a surprise inspection. What then?"

"What then? We pray harder, I suppose." Anna understood her friend's fear, but being interrogated by the Gestapo had become a common experience for those outside convent life. Walking down the street, encountering German officers at a store, or waiting in line for their ration coupons. Anna had not grown used to the experience but had learned how to act around German soldiers, so she didn't raise suspicions.

"Of course, I must pray with more urgency." Sister Aniela blushed, embarrassed that a nun should be reminded to pray. "The monsignor is in the receiving room, so you can go right in. I need to feed the chickens."

Sister Aniela hesitated, her hand still resting on the wooden window frame as a flicker of reflection came to mind. How differently their lives had unfolded. Anna had grown up in a strong, loving family and had always been the brightest pupil in their little school, the one teachers praised and classmates admired. Even now, barely into her twenties, she carried herself with a maturity and steadiness that set her apart. Anna was certainly more responsible, more sensible than most women her age. Aniela was certain that, when the war finally ended, Anna would take her place among those who helped rebuild their country. By comparison, she suddenly felt much younger, almost like the schoolgirl she had once been beside Anna. She smiled warmly. "It's been wonderful to see you, Anna. I hope we can talk later."

As Anna stepped through the convent's front door, her face lit up at the sight of the children. Colin and Elise weren't complete strangers, but she had only just learned about them. The tales Father Kurek had shared of their future adventures had already sparked a sense of family. Now, seeing them in person made those stories feel entirely real.

Elise ran to her and wrapped her in a hug. "Anna, I'm so happy to see you. Maybe we can work together again!"

"Hello, Elise. You must forgive me. I'm still so amazed about your story, but it must be true."

Anna's pleasant demeanor washed away all of Naomi's worries. "I'm Naomi. I'm a Girl Guide, too, just like you! Look, I brought my scout backpack from America."

Anna hugged Naomi before looking in the pack. "A fellow Girl Guide. Let's see what's in it!" Anna wanted to make Naomi feel welcome, but also wondered what a Girl Guide in America might think was important to put in the pack.

Naomi fumbled through her backpack and displayed every item ceremoniously. "Here's a flashlight, matches, a compass, a first aid kit, a bottle of water, trail mix, bug spray, and a map of Ohio. Oh, and sunscreen, extra clothing, and…" A cell phone fell onto the table.

Naomi did a double-take and jumped up and down. "Look! My cell phone! It was in my rain jacket!"

"This is such a relief. I've been wondering how we'd get back to the future. My cellphone battery is so low, but you have one!" Colin smiled widely and laughed. "I always wondered why your parents ever gave such a little kid your own cellphone, but now, I'm really glad they did."

"It was Auntie Wilma who gave it to me." Naomi wrinkled her nose to correct her cousin. "For Christmas."

"Let's see this phone." Anna knelt next to Naomi to inspect this small, mysterious device. "Father Kurek described it when he told me about you, but I just couldn't envision what it must look like. So, this is a phone from the future?"

Monsignor Dunajecki and Sister Roberta walked through the wooden doorframe and greeted Anna.

"Anna, you're here! Have you met the children from America yet? Sister Roberta and I can't tell if they are around. We so wish we could see them!"

"Oh, yes. We've been getting to know one another." Anna prompted Naomi to show them the phone. "Look, Naomi has one of those phones from the future. It's just as Father Kurek described."

"Unfortunately, the phone is just like the children. We can't see any of them." Sister Roberta's lips wrinkled in disappointment.

"Anna, let's tell the children your plans to see if they're willing to help." Monsignor Dunajecki waved his hands for everyone to be seated around the heavy wooden table.

Anna placed her elbows on the table and rested her chin on her balled-up hands. "Children, we have a very serious situation in nearby Kolbuszowa. The Germans forced the Jews to move out of their homes and live in the ghetto areas of the town for the past two years. Now, the Germans will soon send them all to a prison camp in a city about an hour away. Those in the greatest danger are the elderly and the young, since they can't work. Sadly, the Germans view anyone who can't work as an expendable burden."

"Maybe they have a daycare center for the babies?" Naomi asked.

Elise couldn't believe how much Naomi still had to learn. She whispered to Naomi, "No, they are horrible to little kids. They might kill them."

Monsignor Dunajecki's voice became deadly serious. "Children, this isn't going to be as easy as the baby we brought to the convent yesterday."

Sister Roberta made the sign of the cross. "What we

are telling you is that many of the youngest Jewish children will be taken from their parents and killed if we don't help. I'm sorry you have to learn of these things, children, but that's the reality of what is going on. The Germans here are like the Devil himself."

Colin, Elise, and Naomi sat stone-faced and rigid in their chairs. "So, is there some way we can help these babies from the ghetto?" Elise asked.

"Yes, we need to come up with a plan for you to rescue as many babies as we can manage, not just one at a time. Father Kurek and I will be with you," Anna said.

"Will we take the babies to the convent like we did with Pawel?" Naomi asked.

Anna shook her head. "Yes, we'll bring them to the convent. The sisters and I will hide them here, that is, until we can find families who are willing to take them."

"If the villagers are like my relatives in Niwiska, I'm sure they'll be willing to help. Jadwiga, Maria, and Józef are the nicest people I've ever met," Elise said.

Anna moved to sit between the girls. "Rescuing them is actually easier than finding people to take the babies into their homes. Here in Poland, anyone who helps to rescue a Jew is killed on the spot. It doesn't matter if the person they save is an adult or a baby. No prison, no trial. They are shot."

Father Kurek said, "Not only that, children. Everyone living in their homes will also be killed. We priests and nuns are in a better position to be brave because we have no families living with us. Of course, everyone living in this convent or the priest's house is also at risk." The priest hesitated, not wanting to remind Sister Roberta of the fate she understood very well. "All these nuns here would be killed if the Germans found out we were giving shelter to a Jew."

"We will need to have all of the sisters agree before proceeding," the Monsignor said. "Before we ask the sisters, we need you, children, to decide if you are willing to help."

"Of course, we're willing to help. The Germans can't see us, so we are safe," Colin said.

The Monsignor put his hand on Colin's shoulder. "Think through this carefully, children. While you may be safe, any missteps on your part may be enough reason to kill those of us the Germans can see."

Chapter Seven

The Next Mission

After the two priests left, Colin, Elise, and Naomi walked outside with Anna. Anna put her arms around the girls. "Monsignor and Sister Roberta will understand if you children consider this too risky an operation. It's a huge decision."

Elise and Colin glanced into each other's eyes and immediately knew their answer. "Naomi, this is going to be up to you. Colin and I went through things last time that were just as dangerous, but we're not going to lie. Those months in 1944 were the scariest times in my entire life and will probably be the scariest until I'm an old lady. I had never been more terrified than when Noah and I stole food from the Germans' warehouse and thought a German shepherd dog was going to tear us apart."

"Naomi, the hardest thing for you will be to follow orders. Elise and I were once part of the Polish underground army. We swore our loyalty and pledged we were willing to sacrifice our lives for the mission given to us. Can you really say you are willing to die for these babies?" Colin asked.

Anna wrapped her arms gently around Naomi, sensing both her eagerness and her inexperience. "Naomi, you're still so young," she said softly. "Perhaps it would be wiser to remain here at the convent for now. Helping with the babies is important work, too. They would be blessed to have your care, and you'd be such a help around the convent."

"No," Naomi said quickly, her eyes shining with both determination and a hint of pleading. "I want to be with my cousins. I'll follow every order and won't complain. Not even if I'm tired or hungry. Please let me be with them. I can be helpful, you'll see."

"But, can you keep secrets, Naomi? I know how hard that is. That's what I'm most worried about," Elise said. "It's not just about you being weak, but me too."

Instead of her typical sneer, Naomi lowered her eyes. "If another person's life depends on me keeping quiet and following orders, I promise on the Bible. I'll be brave and courageous, just like you guys. I promise!"

Colin inspected his young cousin with the intensity of an eagle. "I think Naomi's quickly growing up. She used to burst into tears at the drop of a hat."

Elise hugged her young cousin. "I know Naomi can do this. Anyway, we all have to stay together, especially when the cell phones start to run low."

"No way can we leave one another behind," Colin said slyly. "If two came back with one of us missing, our parents would kill us when we got back home."

Anna put her arm around Naomi and stroked her chocolate brown hair. "Naomi understands things much better now. Elise and Colin, you two have to remember that you never actually witnessed the Germans beat or kill anyone. We'd all like to think we would be brave. I've witnessed and lived under their brutality. None of us can truly say we would withstand torture and react perfectly. As much as I would like to think I would be brave, I fully admit that I couldn't guarantee it. A person doesn't really know until they are tested."

The children looked at one another with sober eyes. "So, we all agree to help?" Elise asked.

After each signaled agreement, Anna leaned forward to huddle with the children. "Father Kurek will come to the convent tomorrow to bring you to Kolbuszowa. Bring every piece of fabric to wrap the babies in so the Germans can't see them. And Naomi, that backpack of yours may actually hold a baby, so you need to bring it."

Naomi beamed, "We can wrap one in my rain gear, too! I can carry two babies since I'm so strong. One in my backpack and one in the jacket!"

"Naomi, I remember being a Girl Guide when I was your age. We learned so many useful things in the Guides—how to give first aid, survival skills, and how to use a compass in the forest. As soon as the war broke out, the underground army saw how useful the Girl Guides could be. We were asked to deliver important documents, underground newspapers, and help the wounded. Now, we Girl Guides who are older are helping to rescue Jewish babies and children and even committing acts of sabotage."

"What's sabotage?" Naomi asked.

"Women are not usually involved with direct fighting, but if we can do something to destroy or undermine the Germans, we Girl Guides don't hesitate to take action."

"Have you done anything really scary, Anna?" Elise asked.

Anna raised her eyebrows. "If I told you that information, I would be breaking my AK pledge, now, wouldn't I? You have to remember: only those in your cell should know about your activities and your code name."

"Like a cell phone cell?" Naomi asked.

"No, your cell is like a small group to which you belong. Your Home Army cell includes me, the Monsignor, Father Kurek, and now Sister Roberta. Even the other sisters in this convent aren't to know. It is up to Sister Roberta to tell them only what they need to know. That helps to keep our cell safe."

Colin smirked. "Everyone in a cell has a codename. I'm Goon, and Elise is Firecracker."

Anna wrinkled her forehead. I know what a firecracker is, but what's a goon?"

"A goon is the enforcer in ice hockey. Things can get a little rough out there on the ice," Colin chuckled. "A goon makes sure everyone is doing their job."

"I'll need a new codename, won't I?" Naomi asked, jumping up and down with excitement. "How about Moana? Grandma says I look like Moana from the movie."

Anna burst into laughter. "Moana is a perfect name, then. I doubt anyone else in the AK has that name!"

Elise nodded her head in agreement. "Anna, I'm so glad we have someone like you who knows what they're doing."

Anna raised her eyebrows and sighed. "You need to understand that rescuing babies is new to me, also. I hope I don't let you or the babies down."

The girls put their arms around Anna, and Naomi whispered. "You seem pretty perfect to me."

Anna kissed each child on the cheek. "You are too generous with your confidence in me. Remember that

Sister Roberta has to secure each of the nuns' consent to help before we plan anything. We'll have to wait for each sister's agreement."

Chapter Eight

The Nuns' Agreement

Sister Roberta understood the risk of rescuing Jewish babies. The Germans had warned all the convents near Camp Heidelager not to assist the Jews. The soldiers had already searched every crevice in the convent. So far, the sisters had only given shelter to orphaned Polish children. Fortunately, kind local families offered to provide a home for these children. Rescuing Jewish babies had many more obstacles. Some children were safer to rescue than others. They had to have the "right look." Luckily, most infants didn't yet have pronounced Semitic features. Of course, the circumcision of a Jewish baby boy couldn't be easily hidden.

That afternoon, Sister Roberta summoned the sisters to gather around the long wooden table in the quiet dining hall. Sunlight streamed through the high windows, casting flickering lights across the worn pages of her Bible. She opened it to a page marked with a faded silk ribbon and lifted her eyes to them. Her voice was calm and steady, yet tinged with the seriousness of what she was about to ask of them.

"My dear sisters, I read to you from the Gospel of Saint John: *This is my commandment, that you love one another as I have loved you. No one can have greater love than to lay down his life for his friends.*"

The sisters sat expressionless, thinking the scripture was part of their devotions. They did not yet understand what Sister Roberta was about to ask of them.

"What I'm about to discuss will put each of you and our community in great danger. Monsignor Dunajecki has asked us if our convent would give shelter to some of the Jewish babies from the Kolbuszowa ghetto."

The nun then set the holy book on the table. "I am asking each of you to consider if you are willing to be part of this rescue. If not, I will ask a neighboring convent to shelter you while the Sisters of St. Joseph are protecting the Jewish babies."

There was complete silence. No one stirred or glanced up to see the others' reactions. Sister Roberta sat at the head of the table with closed eyes, her hands folded over her Bible. The silence was overwhelming. In her heart, she freely admitted fear for her own life, the lives of so many sisters, and the community. Was it prudent to risk their lives for a few Jewish babies?

When Sister Aniela rose from her seat, the others thought she was signaling her displeasure with the idea, but then she asked to speak. "I can only speak for myself. We have lived for three years under the German occupation of Poland, and we've all seen the worst of humanity. Now we are being asked to save some innocent Jews." The young nun's eyes misted, and a single tear fell down her cheek. "I am sad to say that I was raised with hatred for the Jews. My father claimed the Jewish moneylenders stole his lumber mill from him. Of course, God rest his soul; I must admit the truth. Father drank too much at the Jews' taverns and foolishly gambled away our family's only real possession."

The other nuns looked up in suspense as Sister

Roberta walked over to Sister Aniela and put her arms around the young nun. "We all understand about these things that happened in the past. There's no shame in not wanting to sacrifice your very life."

"No! You don't understand. My father's sins and foolishness were wrong, and it would be an even greater sin for me to say no to a Jewish baby." Sister Aniela clutched the crucifix that hung from her neck. "After all, we all have to die sometime. Why should it not be to rescue an innocent Jewish baby?"

Inspired by the youngest member in the convent, the other nuns' eyes brightened. They all agreed to move forward and nodded confidently with the plan to help rescue the Jewish children.

"But, there's one thing that is a puzzlement to me. I've seen three children here at the convent. Sometimes with the Monsignor and sometimes with Anna Grabiec. They appear to be Polish children, not Jews. No one else seems to notice them. Is my mind playing tricks on me?"

Sister Roberta's eyes glared at Sister Aniela, who wasn't supposed to break that confidence. "Sister Aniela has met the children. Has anyone else here also seen three children?" Sister Roberta asked. The other sisters glanced around the table to gauge each other's reactions to Sister Aniela's bizarre observation and nodded their heads.

Sister Roberta smiled. "Sister Aniela hasn't been hallucinating, but the truth is just as unbelievable as a dream. I tell you the truth. Those children are from the future, and to make the situation more confusing, they are Sister Aniela's blood relatives. Only people who are related by blood can see them."

Sister Agata shuddered. "Could they be demons,

Sister Roberta?"

The nun's collective utterances quickly silenced Sister Agata's foolish assessment.

"Sisters, our very existence these many years has been to be God's blessing to those in need. Neither the children nor this convent ever went out seeking danger, but it has now come to us. Our veils and habits will do little to save us, and I fear the children's invisibility might not be enough to save them either."

"So, we are agreed that it is our duty as followers of Jesus Christ to save the Jewish babies?" Sister Roberta said. All the nuns signaled their willingness. "He is smiling down on all of you right now. Bless you."

Chapter Nine

The Mission

That morning, the sun's intense light was filtered by the tree foliage on each side of the path as Father Kurek pulled back on the reins for the horse to stop. "You can rest under this shady tree, Wojciech."

Father Kurek tied the horse to a post and stroked its mane. "You can get down now, children, but be sure that magical cloth is with you."

Colin, Elise, and Naomi peered from the hay-filled cart near the woods' edge next to the cemetery and then jumped from the edge. Naomi beamed with excitement. "Don't worry, Father Kurek! I have my backpack and my cell phone just in case we get lost."

"Father Kurek, why isn't the Monsignor coming to help us with the babies?" Elise asked.

"Monsignor Dunajecki asked to meet with the Germans to discuss the parish's running a food kitchen for the Jews. He thought it might be helpful for the Nazis to be distracted in the center of town, far from the cemetery. A very wise man. Anyway, the monsignor might not be helpful on this rescue since he can't see you. We need to be as silent as possible."

"I still don't understand how all this is going to work," Colin said. "But, we made sure the blankets couldn't be seen. We did a magic show for some of the nuns at the convent with Anna's help to be sure we were invisible."

Father Kurek helped Naomi and Elise down from the wagon. "Anna and I have never done this before either, so we aren't totally sure. You three must wrap each baby in the blankets we've torn into large strips. Don't let any part of the babies show."

"Won't they cry if we do that?" Naomi asked.

"Very wise, young Naomi." Father Kurek nervously wiped the sweat from his brow. "Babies will cry no matter what we do, and that's why the next part is so important." He then took a paper bag out of his sack. "Naomi, you're in charge of these sugar cubes since you have your scout pack. Place one cube in each baby's mouth as soon as possible."

"Sugar cubes for babies?" Elise said. "Sugar isn't good for babies."

"Anna put a sleeping agent into each cube. Like a medicine. It's so crucial the babies don't cry," Father Kurek said. "Their very lives, and ours, depend on their silence."

The priest handed the bag of sugar cubes to Naomi, who beamed at the responsibility. "You can see the cemetery is to the left. Anna should be at the back of the priests' house next to the church. Have the coverings ready and hide the babies behind this huge tombstone after Naomi gives them the cubes. Each of you should take two children to the wagon and wait for all of us to return. We'll take the same road to the north to get back to the convent. That way, we can avoid going through the town."

The priest strolled inconspicuously through the cemetery as the three children trailed behind him. To the south, they could hear the sound of cars and trucks and observed the tiny figures of people moving around the town. Hopefully, the children were still invisible to any German soldier who might happen to see them.

The small rescue party scanned the cemetery but noticed no sign of Anna.

"Look! A hand is waving behind a gravestone," whispered Colin. "That has to be Anna."

The children ran towards Anna as Father Kurek slowly strolled to avoid any suspicion.

"Naomi, these two are becoming restless. We need those sugar cubes." Anna kept making the sign of the cross. "I'm obviously no good at calming babies."

Naomi retrieved two cubes and put them in each baby's mouth. "Oh, some of it is leaking out of their mouth!" She scraped the crystalline drool back into their mouths and then shuddered. "Eww! Baby spit."

Father Kurek retrieved two wooden toolboxes he had hidden behind another grave. "I drilled holes in these, so the two I carry can breathe easily.

Anna placed two of the children inside and closed the wooden lid. "Elise, hide behind the cemetery's stone wall with the babies until Colin has his two, and both of you go and wait at the wagon. The others are just beyond that building with the broken door."

Elise shivered with fear despite the warm summer temperatures as she cradled an exceptionally fussy one. "Don't cry, baby. Please don't cry!" she pleaded.

Naomi quickly sedated and wrapped the remaining children.

Anna discreetly scanned the surroundings, carefully examining the area to ensure there were no prying eyes focused on their activities. She then turned to Naomi.

"Okay, let's get out of here. You go as quickly as possible, Naomi. Father Kurek and I have to walk slowly so we don't attract attention. Be sure the babies are hidden under the hay."

Naomi darted across the cemetery to join her cousins at the wagon with one baby in her small but strong arms and the other safely tucked into her backpack. "I did it!" Naomi sighed and then handed her bundles to her cousins.

"Let's first take the wrappings off their faces," Elise suggested.

Father Kurek soon joined them, carrying two heavy toolboxes and a seemingly stuffed rucksack. "Three more for the hay." He lifted the babies into the awaiting arms of the two girls. "Anna has already taken off on her bicycle with a baby in her sack. She'll meet us at the convent."

Colin joined the priest on the wagon's bench, and the girls sat amidst the drowsy babies on the hay. "Mission accomplished! We can get out of this town. All those Germans down the street didn't seem to suspect a thing. The monsignor did a great job providing a distraction for our mission."

Wojciech, the monsignor's old horse, waited patiently with his head down, unaware of his part in this dangerous task. He lifted his head as Father Kurek untied the reins. "Let's go, Wojciech!" was all the horse needed to hear.

The little conveyance moved swiftly, carrying the four rescuers and their precious cargo down the dirt path into the shadows of the forest. Colin turned to see the girls embracing one another. "I can't believe you each carried two of those heavy babies. You guys did good."

The atmosphere was filled with a sense of relief as the foursome exchanged congratulatory glances, their faces breaking into relieved smiles. They couldn't help but feel a surge of satisfaction, as their hard work had been successful.

The group's relief was short-lived. In the distance, a man's silhouette stood against the shafts of sunlight filtering through the trees. As he drew closer, he began waving wildly.

"Father Kurek! You have young guests today! What is the special occasion?"

"Mishka, good to see you!" The priest silently prayed for the composure to mask his unease. Mishka was the kind of man who repelled others at first glance. His rough speech, coarse mannerisms, and snarling face were made worse by a thick layer of unshaven stubble.

When his sharp, predatory eyes fixed on the three children, a cold wave of fear washed over them. Everything about him—his voice, his expression—marked him as evil.

Mishka plucked the cigarette from his lips, exhaled a cloud of smoke, and bellowed, "Children, you are strangers!" The words carried an unmistakable edge of malice, easily recognized by anyone who knew him.

The children sat frozen, clinging to the hope that Father Kurek would handle the exchange. Thankfully, the priest's mind went straight to the cover story the Monsignor had prepared for just such a moment.

"These children are orphans from Sandomierz. Their father was a Polish officer, and their mother hasn't been found. I'm taking them to Mielec to meet up with their uncle, who'll take them to his home in Zawoja."

Mishka twisted his mouth and closed one eye as he

inspected their faces. "It seems suspicious nowadays that most orphans have fathers who were Polish officers." With a wicked grin, he decided to test them. "Children, let me hear you say your prayers. Ask for God's protection. Right now."

Colin nodded for Elise and Naomi to join him. They bowed their heads and put their hands in prayer position just like their great-grandmother Jadwiga Bryk had taught them, which now seemed so long ago.

"Our Father, Who art in heaven, hallowed be Thy name; Thy kingdom come; Thy will be done on earth as it is in heaven. Give us this day our daily bread, and forgive us our trespasses as we forgive those who trespass against us; and lead us not into temptation, but deliver us from evil. Amen."

Mishka narrowed his eyes and tilted his head as he came closer to inspect Naomi. "The little one was not so sure of her prayers. Perhaps she was not raised so good a Catholic."

Father Kurek clasped the horses' reins so tight that his knuckles turned white, and he bit his lip to subdue his anger. "Mishka, these children have lost their parents. How can you say such things? Can you imagine the horrors they have lived through these past months?" With a dismissive wave of his hand, Father Kurek clicked the reins as the horse galloped past Mishka. "Go home and repent."

Once safely past Mishka, Elise said, "Whew! That was a close one! Another person who could see us!"

"That also means we're related to that jerk," Colin sputtered.

"You can't choose your relatives, children. Many will disappoint." Father Kurek kept taking heavy breaths to calm himself.

Naomi's tears began to flow onto the dry hay. "I don't know how to pray in Polish as well as Colin and Elise. I ruined everything."

Elise wrapped her arms around her sobbing cousin. "No, no. Naomi. You performed as well as any AK partisan. We're all very proud of you."

Father Kurek tried to console Naomi. "That's for certain. You should all receive a medal for your bravery." He also knew his face mustn't betray his fears about Mishka to the children. Mishka, that scoundrel, will surely report the sighting of the children to the Germans. He would need to talk with the monsignor right away.

Chapter Ten

Success

The rhythmic clip-clop of Wojciech's hooves
alerted the sisters that the rescuers had arrived. Sister
Roberta waved them in and locked the wooden gate
behind them. "Praise Jesus; you're back. Did everything
go as planned?"

"We have a wagon full of babies from the ghetto,
thanks to these marvelous children. Yes, I suppose you
could say everything went as planned." Father Kurek
kept the story of Mishka to himself for the time being.

Colin jumped off the bench and helped the girls pass
the sleeping babies off to the nuns. The sisters whisked
the babies into the chapel, where they had brought
drawers from their dresser bureaus to use as cribs. Each
bed was lined with every available cloth and rag the
sisters could find, including some of their extra black
habits.

So far, this part of their mission was a success.
Everyone stood quietly inside the chapel in amazement.
Then Sister Roberta went forward to the altar and went
down on her knees to give thanks to God. One by one,
the others followed, sinking to their knees in quiet
thanksgiving.

The bells' clanging signaled Anna's arrival. The
girls ran up to her as she slipped through the front door

with her bundle. Elise brought the baby to the remaining bed and unraveled some of the blanket strips. "Listen! This one is waking up, I think," whispered Elise to Naomi.

"Anna, what is this one's name?" asked Naomi.

"From this moment on, all the babies will have new names. It's for everyone's safety."

Father Kurek leaned down to inspect the child. "It's best if we describe each baby as a foundling a villager discovered in the forest, or in an abandoned Polish home."

Sister Roberta signaled for the three children to sit in the pews with her and Anna. "You have had quite an education these past few days, haven't you? Now, we must tell untrue stories, lie, and do the unthinkable to deceive the enemies. We'll do everything possible to protect their identities as Jews."

Furrowed lines etched themselves across Colin's brow. "How will their parents ever find them when the war ends?"

Father Kurek answered, "Anna has written down their parents' names and the children's birth dates and will bury them in the field near the barn. We can't have any records in the convent in case the Germans come to search...and they will."

Anna placed the murmuring infant in Naomi's arms. "As the months progress, we'll learn which ones have passable features and which ones will need more protection."

"What does passable mean? I'm still confused," Elise said.

"Their hair may be too dark to pass; one may develop a Semitic nose and cheekbones," Anna said.

Father Kurek said. "Fortunately, these babies don't know the Jewish prayers or practices. They can't give away the secrets they don't even yet know. Children who have learned to talk present grave dangers for their rescuers."

"Different Jewish prayers, I understand. What do you mean by practices?" Elise asked.

"Jewish people around here dress differently and do things like cross themselves three times before they eat. Sometimes, a child will speak and blurt out in Yiddish if they are frightened. In this way, even a two-year-old can reveal their true identity to the Germans." Father Kurek said.

"So, they'll learn the Catholic prayers and go to church instead of the synagogue when they get older?" Colin asked.

"Everything is in God's hands. The war could end soon, and their parents may still be alive. Then the babies can go back to their real parents and learn the Jewish way of living." Father Kurek said.

"We had to recite our prayers for that nasty man who stopped us from passing." Naomi began to tear up again, just thinking about Mishka. "I need to do a better job of learning my prayers. He called me a bad Catholic girl."

Anna whispered to Sister Roberta about the children's encounter with Mishka. "What's this? You ran into Mishka?" the nun asked.

"Yes, Mishka." Father Kurek's eyes grew wide. "He's just a nasty old man, Naomi. Don't think anything of it." The priest then tipped his head to signal that a private conversation was needed. Sister Roberta followed him to a spot near the confessionals.

The priest's voice lowered, "We had the misfortune

of running into Mishka. He seemed suspicious of Naomi. Maybe it was her olive skin, but Mishka demanded the children say their prayers. Naomi did a good job, but that man is a szmalcownik, a traitor. Always looking to see if he can make his pockets grow richer by feeding information to the Gestapo."

The nun covered her mouth and whispered, "Father, Mishka is Sister Aniela's brother. You are right that he's a scoundrel, just like his alcoholic father."

"Mishka will likely be prowling around the convent or the priest's house to check on the children's whereabouts." It wasn't often that anger got the best of Father Kurek, but now he was seething in anger. "Let me know immediately if you see him around here, pumping his sister with questions. There's no one more dangerous to the safety of our American children than Mishka."

Chapter Eleven

Max

The forest was hot and still. Not a single breeze stirred a solitary leaf in the trees. Max removed his cap and wiped the sweat off his brow, glad to be alone for a moment of peace. He then heard the rustle of leaves. A hunched worker from his workgroup appeared from behind the pile of freshly felled logs. "Are you coming with us?"

From a distance, Max saw a group of laborers running into the woods. It appeared they were trying to escape. "Yeah, uh, sure," not knowing what else to say. That was all Max needed to join his fellow Jewish prisoners. He didn't even know their names.

Max grabbed his jacket and rucksack and ran with the group down a gnarly path deep into the forest wilderness. "Where are we going?"

"Jakob says there are refugees from town hiding out nearby. We'll try to find their hideout."

"I thought the Jews only came out at night. How will we ever find them?" Max asked.

"Don't worry. We'll meet up with them. Right now, we only have to worry about food," one of the ragged refugees uttered. "And hiding from the Germans."

The roar of trucks magnified from a distance. "Germans! Scatter!" was all Max heard.

Max bolted into the woods, leaping over the brush and dead tree limbs. His heart pounded, but he kept going until he could run no longer. Four shots echoed from afar. Max's eyes darted from tree to tree to find the others, but he soon realized he was alone.

Trembling, Max collapsed under a tree to consider his options. For now, he needed to stay put as he pondered his situation. He was alone in what Hitler referred to as his "Camp Wilderness." The heavily forested region was swarming with Germans of the worst kind: the highly trained and evil SS. It was the perfect place for the Germans to hide their secret projects. Not only was Heidelager the largest SS training camp outside of Germany, but it also contained Pustkow, a barbaric concentration and extermination camp from which he had just escaped. How could he have been so unlucky?

Max put his hand in his pocket and caressed his mother's final letter, written before her execution at the prison for Jews in Rzeszów. At age fourteen, he had no aunts or uncles left in Kolbuszowa, and a real sense of aloneness and despair suddenly swept over him. Young Max was the only one in his family to have survived. There was no one left who could help him.

It seemed bizarre to Max as he thought of the priest from Kolbuszowa who had left an indelible mark on him. The memory wasn't at all comforting, but the recollection from just a few years prior was now seared into his mind. While attending Kolbuszowa's public school, his Polish teacher complimented his studies to the stately visiting priest, who congratulated Max by patting him on the head. The priest probably didn't realize that Max's Jewish peers would twist this kind gesture. For days after that incident, his Jewish classmates taunted him, "A priest touched you! You're not kosher anymore!" At the time, Max hated that priest. Ironically, that small compliment was now his only connection to a person in Kolbuszowa.

Maybe I can find that priest. Maybe he will help me.

The blazing sun overhead guided Max to find his way through the forest until he reached the outskirts of Kolbuszowa. Max had to bolt into doorways to hide whenever he heard a voice or sound as he walked through the back alleys. Finally, he stood at the bottom of the church and glanced around to see if anyone had taken notice of him.

The long set of steps to All Saints Roman Catholic Church beckoned. Max had never been inside a church, even though this one was a vital part of his hometown. As a yeshiva student, he knew almost nothing about Christian rituals. The Catholic Church was a place where he never had the slightest bit of interest, but then the Catholics felt the same way about the Jews. It seemed peculiar that the only safe place in Kolbuszowa for a Jew was now the inside of the church.

I'll go in just for a minute. Max sought out reasons to rationalize going into a Catholic church. *I need somewhere to cool off.* He again checked for the presence of Germans in the vicinity and opened the heavy wood door. As Max entered the dimly lit church, he noted it was empty. Max walked down the aisle, fascinated by the scenes on the walls. He concluded the artwork must depict the life of Jesus. He thought the woman with the infant at her breast must be Mary. Max also noticed a picture of the Crucifixion and wondered how his rabbi would have described these representations. The Catholics at his school always blamed the Jews for Jesus' death.

Max sat down on a creaky side pew and took off his jacket to hide his yellow star. No longer donning earlocks as he did in his youth, Max was relieved he now looked more like a Pole. At least he wouldn't draw attention to himself in case anyone came in.

Alone and in silence, Max sat for maybe ten minutes and was about to stand up when he felt a hand descend on his right shoulder. He had heard no footsteps, no breathing, nothing. Whoever this was kept his hand on Max's shoulder. The Gestapo or some German official? Max thought. My punishment for being in a forbidden place?

Instead, Max turned to see the kind face of the same priest who had once complimented his academic accomplishment. That event now seemed so long ago, and Max was immediately ashamed of his previous impertinent thoughts. "My son," the priest asked softly, "are you hungry?" Max nodded, and the priest gestured to follow him.

Max walked up the church's aisle behind this giant man and then down a corridor filled with statues and religious pictures. They entered a room not much larger than a closet.

"Wait here. It's safe." The priest returned with a bowl of potato soup. "I'm Monsignor Dunajecki," he said, handing Max the bowl, spoon, and piece of dark bread. "Eat in peace." Max squatted on the floor and mopped the bowl with the bread so that not one speck of soup remained.

"Are you from this area?" asked the priest. Max didn't know if he could trust him. Would he be handed over to the Gestapo, or would the priest show some mercy? At least, Max thought, I'll meet my fate on a full stomach.

"My name is Max. Before the war, my father was the currency manager at the bank here in Kolbuszowa. I have no family. Everyone was killed in Rzeszow."

"Did you escape from that camp?"

"No, I just escaped from the Jewish labor camp at Pustkow."

"That was very risky! The Gestapo will be searching for you, and Kolbuszowa may be the worst place for you to hide."

"You're right. All the Jews from the ghetto are being taken to Rzeszow. Soon, no one will be left who could help me." Max hung his head and let out a hard sigh. "I can't survive on my own in the forests with the AK partisans and gangs of criminals roaming about."

"Son, you spent your whole young life in this town. Surely, someone will recognize you, although I must say you could easily pass for a Roman Catholic boy with your good looks and your fine command of the Polish language."

Max cringed hearing the term "good looks" as Jews were either described as having the good looks of a Pole or the 'bad, Semitic look of a Jew.' Max stood nervously in front of the priest with desperation etched on his face. "Can you help me? I'm strong and will work day and night if some farmer allows me to hide in his barn."

Seeing the fatigue and despair in Max's eyes, Monsignor Dunajecki nodded, "For now, you can stay in the attic of the rectory. Tomorrow, we'll decide what to do." The priest patted Max on his shoulder. This time, Max perceived the pat as comforting and much appreciated.

Chapter Twelve

What to Do with Max?

Monsignor Dunajecki slumped in his chair and sighed. As he leaned back, the priest admired the desk that had seen better days since being made by some long-forgotten wood maker from Kolbuszowa. He rubbed his hand over the ornate detailing of the wood. That skilled man from the 1800s had plenty of problems of his own, but most likely sat alone in his little workshop without scores of desperate, hungry people asking for his help. The monsignor felt crushed under his numerous daily responsibilities. Feeding hundreds of hungry Jews and Poles in Kolbuszowa, meeting his parishioners' spiritual needs, and also the faithful from the surrounding villages. Now, more Jewish children to protect.

Dunajecki's experience in prison during the first week of the German occupation taught him a hard lesson: the Germans were suspicious of everyone, including the clergy. The occupiers wanted to instill terror in the population and wouldn't exempt their parish priest from a few days in prison.

No one could talk their way out of the Germans' commands for long. The Jews continually tried to bribe the occupiers for small favors, but any favor was only temporary. In reality, their strategy only backfired. The Germans assumed the Jews had unlimited access to cash, gold, furs, and expensive art they had effectively hidden in obscure places.

The door to the study creaked open, and Father Kurek entered. "Eva said you wanted to see me."

The Monsignor signaled for the young priest to be seated. In the past several years, the older priest had developed a close relationship with his young protégé. Having another colleague in his home was comforting during this time of great stress and need. "Jan, we can't keep Max here at the rectory. The Germans create all kinds of excuses to enter with their spontaneous inspections. I'm going to ask Sister Roberta if she would keep him or help find a home in one of the villages to the north, where the Germans aren't swarming like here in Kolbuszowa."

Before speaking, Father Kurek's thoughts churned with frustration and dread. Each day, the presence of the Germans seemed to tighten its grip on the town like a vice. He remembered quieter years, when the square outside the church in Kolbuszowa bustled with farmers' chatter and the clatter of market stalls, not the snap of boots on cobblestones or the harsh guttural commands of officers. The Gestapo headquarters now loomed like a dark shadow over the parish. The sight outside, with a jarring mix of sleek military cars and worn wooden carts, reminded him of how the occupiers had intruded into every corner of life.

"Antoni, how did we get to be so unfortunate to have most of the German commanders from Camp Heidelager right here in town with the Gestapo headquarters across the street from the church?" Father Kurek glared at the building out the window and noted the mixture of German vehicles and the horse and carts of the Poles.

"You're right. It's much too dangerous for a Jew from Kolbuszowa to stay here."

"If Max were discovered, the Germans would retaliate against not only us but also the entire congregation. I can't sacrifice innocent people here in town."

"We'll take him to the convent tomorrow after mass. Of course, the American children are there too, but he won't be able to see them because he's a Jew," Father Kurek said.

"Yes, Jan. Max will also be much happier in the countryside, even though he's a city boy. He needs some peace."

"Why don't I ride my bike to the convent to see if Sister Roberta will agree?" Father Kurek smiled. "How did we priests get tasked with helping to run an orphanage?"

The following day, Monsignor Dunajecki joined Max on a weathered wooden bench in the convent's courtyard. He gestured toward the scene before them. "Look over there, Max. Under the shade of this old oak, the sisters have created a haven of beauty. Flowers in full bloom, neatly tended plants. Such a peaceful place to rest one's soul."

Max's face flushed, and he sprang up. His heart began hammering like it belonged to a rabbit being chased by a fox. Not from heat or fatigue but from fear. "There are babies here; I can hear the crying of babies."

Monsignor Dunajecki paused, trying to construct a believable answer that would calm Max. "Yes, those children are foundlings the villagers discovered in the forest. Many nearby villages were forced to evacuate. Parents, desperate, traveled long distances to beg a relative to take their children. Some had no choice but to leave their own babies behind. They knew the sisters here would care for them."

"But I didn't know anyone else besides nuns would be here." Max's face became sullen, and he shouted. "I thought you could guarantee me a safe place. A convent with babies isn't safe! I know. I lived in the ghetto with screaming babies for almost two years!"

The monsignor blew out a deep breath and stared at the young man. "Do you think you're the only one with problems? The Germans have killed hundreds of Poles here in Kolbuszowa, along with the Jews. All the Poles are on rations, just like the Jews. They also live in constant fear of their families being killed."

Max cocked his head with the arrogant intention of giving the priest a history lesson. "The Jews have it so much worse than the Poles. From the first day of occupation, the Poles pointed out where the Jews lived and which ones of us were Jews so the Germans could take everything we had."

"Max, you're an intelligent boy. Think about these accusations of yours. The Germans didn't need our help to uncover who was Jewish. Most Jews have Semitic features, and those in Kolbuszowa dress very differently from Poles. Anyone with a brain can figure out who is a Jew and who is a Pole in this town. And remember, most of the Kolbuszowa Jews don't speak Polish or German, just Yiddish."

Max bowed his head sheepishly and nodded in agreement.

"These nuns are risking their lives by sheltering you. They share their meager food rations with you." The monsignor's eyes blazed, and he now doubted the wisdom of helping out this young man who might betray his rescuers. "Remember this. It takes ten Poles to save a Jew but only one Jew to destroy a hundred Poles if that Jew betrays those who help him."

Max thought back to the conversations he overheard all his life. The Jewish community in Kolbuszowa lived separately from the Gentiles, whom they referred to as "goys." It wasn't that they didn't get along; it was that no one ever really tried. Most personal exchanges were civil, even what Max considered friendly. Jews were taught they were God's chosen people and should shun associating with Gentiles. When tempers flared, a few Polish boys shouted that Jews killed Jesus, but that rarely happened. It seemed everyone just understood it was best to stay with their own kind.

"You're right, Monsignor. There are good and bad in all religions."

Dunajecki lowered his voice and spoke more deliberately. "Then be one of the good ones who appreciates and defends his rescuers. That attitude will do more to save your people than bitterness over a few."

Max's chin dropped to his chest, embarrassed and desperately wanting to change the subject. "Monsignor, who are those Polish children playing in the fields? See? Over there in the fields." Max stood and approached the corner of the small barn to get a closer look.

The Monsignor's cheeks flushed as he shook his head nervously, realizing Max might have spotted the American children. "Um, I'm not sure. Ah, maybe some local children who help the sisters in the fields."

"I can't let them see me!" Max ran frantically to shield his presence from the children.

"Come into the house, Max. I think you'll need first

to meet Sister Roberta before I tell you something quite extraordinary."

After introducing Max to Sister Roberta, Monsignor Dunajecki excused himself. "I'll need to find Father Kurek and have him retrieve the children from the fields."

Moments later, the wooden door of the reception room creaked open. Max heard Father Kurek say from the other room, "Children, there is a person who I think needs to meet you."

Max stood before the three Americans, and his eyebrows furrowed. "Those are the Polish children from the fields. Why are you bringing them in here?"

Monsignor Dunajecki responded. "So. Can you see the children?"

"Of course, I can see them. Two girls and a boy about my age."

Sister Roberta shook her head authoritatively. "Impossible! Max is a Jew!"

"Tell Sister Roberta that maybe he's like Sister Aniela," Naomi said.

"Maybe we are related," Colin whispered to Father Kurek. "Grandma said we had just a little bit of Jewish blood."

It didn't take long for Max to uncover the mystery of the children's invisibility to some people. "So, only people who are related can see you?"

"Sister Roberta and I can't see them, but she and I know they are real." The Monsignor then explained the children's story.

Max glanced around to gauge the adults' reactions and could relate to their wide-eyed expressions of disbelief. "Okay, maybe I am related to you Gentiles, because one of our ancestors married outside the faith?" Max looked down at the ground. "This is very strange because you're dressed the same as the Poles in Kolbuszowa. Pretty wealthy ones, too."

"Monsignor Dunajecki thought it was important for us to fit in if someone else saw us. You're not the only one who has seen us." Colin said. "These aren't our real clothes.

Naomi twirled around, allowing her colorful skirt to billow in the air. "Monsignor said we should tell others we're the children of a Polish army officer."

Father Kurek raised his eyebrows and stared directly at Naomi, "Maybe someone needs to be more careful with their secrets?" He chuckled and kept his gaze right on Naomi. "Now, I'm not directing that comment at anyone in particular…Naomi."

Naomi frowned playfully and then hugged the young priest.

Father Kurek bent down to embrace Naomi. "Max, we have our darling Elise, and now we have our precious Naomi. What lucky persons are we!"

Chapter Thirteen

Getting Used to Convent Life

The convent was a perfect but tragic depiction of Poland during the war. Within just three years, it had grown worn and tattered, with a few windows broken and its stone façade crumbling. Yet, despite its present condition, the convent was still inhabited by Godly and courageous people. Just like the country of Poland. Sister Roberta gave encouragement every evening during vespers with the reminder, "What good would this convent and our lives be if, in the end, we had to hide our faces shamefully before the eyes of God?"

The wooden wall bordering the convent gave the illusion of safety. Still, everyone knew the Germans could demand entry at any time of day or night. At the very least, its remote location allowed those inside to have refuge from the raucous Germans' routine military activities in nearby Camp Heidelager. It was also far enough away from the savage concentration camp where Max was once a forced laborer.

Sister Roberta insisted the four children continue their studies under the guidance of Sister Aniela. The four children sat at the table in the dining hall with their journals and ink pens, poised to begin their essays. Creative writing was always the first subject assigned. They all knew the drill—morning chapel and prayers, farm work, lunch, and then school.

Elise carefully filled her fountain pen with ink from the shared bottle. She made a mental note to bring loads of modern ink pens to Poland if she ever returned. "What's weird is how on schedule everything is around here. None of the nuns has a clock except in Sister Roberta's office, yet they know exactly when we should start our school work at 1:00 after lunch."

Colin always started his academic sessions in a huff. "Back home, this is the summertime, and we don't go to school. I've tried to tell Father Kurek that, but he just gives me the same old lecture that I should be grateful."

Max glared at Colin but knew he would feel the same way if the tables were turned. "I haven't been to school in three years. School stopped the day the Germans invaded."

"So, you got to stay home and just watch TV for three years?" Naomi's sparkle faded as she remembered. "Oh, wait. I forgot you don't have any TVs yet."

"I was so foolish, so naïve when the war first started. Last year, I signed up for work detail to show everyone I wasn't a little kid anymore. That I could do men's work." Max's face became sullen and almost teary. "All the Jews in Kolbuszowa thought that if we did what the Germans commanded and gave in to their demands, we would be left alone. That we might be safe, even appreciated."

"So, what are you going to do after the war, Max?" Elise asked. "Do you have a plan to find your family?"

"From what I have seen and heard, everyone is gone. All my family were either killed in Kolbuszowa or were executed in the camp in Rzeszów. I've no one left."

The three children could only utter condolences for

Max but knew they could offer little advice.

"All I have left is a letter my mother sent to me from prison," Max said.

Elise's eyes sparked. "Wait. I know Anna and Father Kurek lived for many years after the war. So did my family, who are still in Niwiska. They could take care of you."

"That might be what I'll do for a while, but I want to go to America after the war and find other Jews who escaped the Germans. Live with them." Max knew it would be hard for the Poles to accept him, even if they acted compassionately. "Maybe I'll go to Israel and live on a kibbutz."

The heavy wooden door swung open, and Sister Aniela entered with a load of books and tablets. "Are you ready for your studies today?" The young nun hadn't revealed that she spent hours every evening attempting to stay one lesson ahead of Elise and Colin.

Sister Aniela stood behind a table in front of the blackboard. She cleared her throat and read directly from her notebook. "Today, we will discuss how to find the perimeter of a right triangle by using the sum of the lengths of the two legs and the hypotenuse."

Colin sighed, unaware that the young nun was also shaky in geometry. "Uh, Sister Aniela, I think you're going to have to back up a bit."

Chapter Fourteen

Rachela

"There, that's the convent." The anxious farmer pointed at a distance to the only two-story building in the village. "Ring the bell. They'll take you in, but don't tell the nuns you're Jewish! And, remember your Polish name, Zosia Dabrowska."

Rachela's tangled blonde hair blew about her face, obscuring the grime broken by the tracks of her tears. She stood frozen in the field of blue cornflowers and scarlet poppies and stared at the man as he ran back into the woods. He couldn't get rid of her soon enough.

Why was I born a person everyone despises? Memories of the last time she had seen her parents flooded over Rachela. Her father disappeared two months ago, and her mother concluded he had been picked up by the Germans. Assuming he was languishing in a concentration camp, her mother struggled in desperation. Sadly, she told Rachela she was going to commit suicide.

This morning, the farmer who had been sheltering Rachela informed her that his family could no longer keep her. The man insisted the Gestapo was hunting for Jews and would search every plank of wood and haystack of the farm in their pursuit of a Jew. His wife disagreed and begged her husband to keep Rachela. "She has the good looks of a Polish child with her blonde hair and blue eyes. The Germans will believe she is our own."

But this had been the pattern of Rachela's life for the past year. Local farmers would take her in for a time, until news spread that Jews had been discovered in the village. Then fear would grip the households, and no amount of money could outweigh the risk of death. In their panic, they would pass her along to someone else, as though she were a burden to be shuffled away.

Seven-year-old Rachela didn't blame the man and was too young to understand that the money for her care had probably run out. His sister had been shot the previous week for the treasonous act of keeping her quern. She refused to comply when the orders were announced that having a simple flour mill was against the law. The Germans learned about her family's support for the partisans in the forests. She and a few other neighbors made extra loaves of bread to deliver to the hungry men. That could only have been possible if she attempted to mill her own flour. The Germans sought to control every aspect of the villagers' lives.

Rachela trudged through the grasses and flowers to the stone path that led to the convent. She hesitated at the gate and had to steady herself when a wave of light-headedness came over her body. Rachela reached for the bell with an unsteady hand. Now that she knew her mother was dead, she had no alternatives except living out in the forests with the wild boars and wolves.

Sister Adolfina opened the gate door's viewing window and then unbolted the gate. "Oh, child. Come, come." With her double chin, rotund middle, and exaggerated waddle, the nun gave every indication she was the convent's cook. The portly woman scanned up and down the path for observers. "Did anyone bring you here?"

"No, my mother died, and I don't know where my father is," Rachela said. Although true, she knew not to convey much more of her situation. Although they had abandoned her, Rachela didn't want to endanger her previous protectors.

Rachela noticed the peaceful vegetable and flower gardens lined with beech hedgerows as they walked through the courtyard. In it nested a community of birds, flittering about and taking shelter in its greenery.

"I'm sure you're hungry. Come into the kitchen." Sister Adolfina hurried Rachela into the kitchen and ladled potato soup into a ceramic bowl. "What is your name?"

"Zosia."

"And your last name?"

"Dabrowska."

"And your parents?"

Rachela replied, "My father is probably dead, but I learned just this morning that my mother is also. I have no one."

Sister Adolfina grimaced and then inspected the poorly dressed child. Shabby boots, a crumpled dress of shepherd's cloth, and a coat made from a blanket. "Sit at this table and eat while I fetch Sister Roberta."

The two nuns hurried back to the kitchen. "Sister Roberta, she speaks Polish, so she must be one of the local children."

Sister Adolfina walked to the counter and cut a slice of black bread for the child.

"Are you from this area, child?" Sister Roberta asked.

"I'm from Mielec."

"Why did you come so far? There is a convent similar to ours right in Mielec." Sister Roberta said.

"I don't know." Rachela's voice trailed off. She kept her gaze on the soup as the nuns moved to the hallway to discuss her situation. A spirit of boldness and desperation arose in the child as she couldn't risk being turned away. "Please! I will work for you. I'll do whatever you like if you'll just let me stay."

Sister Roberta sat next to Rachela. "Child, you're safe here. No one is going to notify the Gestapo. We'll hide you, but we need to know more about you. Do you have papers?"

Rachela's face turned red as she shrugged her shoulders.

Sister Roberta discerned Rachela had been taught to say little. "The monsignor from Kolbuszowa will be here soon. He can provide you with a birth certificate, Zosia Dabrowska. Still, you'll have to tell us what you remember about your parents."

"First, let me help you find clothes that will be more suitable. Such a good thing we were an orphanage and school for children your age before the war. You'll want to look your best for the monsignor." Sister Adolfina gently put her hand in the child's and led her to the storage room. "We'll go over your prayers when you're cleaned up and suitably dressed."

When he arrived, Monsignor Dunajecki didn't have a moment to say more than hello to the other sisters. Sister Roberta hurried him into the reception area. "Monsignor, we have a situation with a foundling. She came to us today. Something isn't right. The child says she's from Mielec but didn't go to the convent there for help. She's also very hesitant to talk, sort of like how a Jewess would act, but she looks and sounds like a Polish child."

Sister Adolfina escorted Zosia into the room. She curtsied and then approached the monsignor when he signaled her to come near. "Good afternoon, Mr. Dunajecki."

The monsignor cleared his throat and glanced at the sisters to assess their reaction to Rachela's greeting. "Good afternoon, Zosia. The good sisters told me you arrived just today, asking for shelter. They say you have no idea of where your parents are."

"My mother is not alive, and I don't know about my father."

"And how did it happen that you came here?"

"I was taken in by some people near Mielec who received some money and linen from my father. They had a girl my age."

So, Zosia, are you really from Mielec?" the monsignor asked.

Rachela wanted to keep up the masquerade but quickly sensed its futility. She squinted and then lowered her brow. Soon, a flood of words came forth. "No, I'm...from L'viv. Another man brought me to the people in Mielec. But then they worried about the Germans breaking into their home to look for me, and I had to leave. The man took me to a field near this convent. He said, "Go straight to that building, and don't talk to anyone along the way. The nuns will take you in."

"Zosia, have you received your First Communion?"

"No, sir, but I know my prayers!" Rachela quickly folded her hands and recited the Lord's Prayer and the Hail Mary without being asked.

The Monsignor was well acquainted with the need for Jewish children to be instructed in Catholic prayers. "Very good. Now, if I were to inquire at the diocese of L'viv, would I find your birth and baptismal records? We have many sisters here at this convent from L'viv, and they could inquire for you to receive a copy."

Rachela flushed, and a lump formed in her throat. "My real name is Rachela Weinstein. I'm from L'viv, though. Everything else is true."

"So, you are Jewish then?"

Rachela's arms fell to her side. "Yes." Tears streamed from her eyes. "I hate being Jewish."

Sister Roberta rushed to Rachela's side. "No. You did nothing wrong. Our Lord Jesus was a Jew. You are one of God's chosen people."

Rachela's quiet demeanor changed to one of defiance. "No, Sister, Catholics hate us because we killed Jesus. Living in this convent is my chance to rid myself, once and for all, of being Jewish." Rachela lowered her voice to a more respectful tone. "I want to be baptized and be a Christian."

Monsignor Dunajecki cocked his head. "Rachela, you said your father still lives. Is that true?"

"I don't know where he is, but my father is wealthy. He paid his employees to keep him in hiding."

"Then it's impossible to baptize you. The war will someday end, and your father will search for you. We only baptize those of whom we are certain have no family at all. That isn't the case with you, Rachela."

Rachela choked through her tears. "But I hate being Jewish. I just want to feel safe instead of hunted."

Monsignor Dunajecki stroked Zosia's hair. "That is our bishop's decision, Zosia. I must follow his rules, just like you must follow all of the sisters' instructions."

Sister Roberta put her arms around the child. "For now, you'll be treated like a Catholic for your safety. Do everything possible to fit in as a Polish girl." The nun stroked the blonde locks on Zosia's head. "Your looks are what will save you, but know that the Gestapo would happily torch this convent and kill everyone if they knew we were hiding Jews."

The monsignor said, "From now on, you will be Zosia, but always embrace your real name. Your Hebrew namesake of Rachel, is one of our most revered Old Testament mothers."

Sister Roberta knelt at Zosia's feet and caressed the child's rough hands. "For now, you will stay in my room. Perhaps, a bit later, I will introduce you to another young person who is staying with us."

Chapter Fifteen

Meeting Zosia

The following day, Max woke up before dawn and looked around the children's sleeping quarters. Everyone was sleeping quietly and calmly, giving him some hope that there was no longer anything for him to fear. Colin always slept with his covers over his head. The girls were on their backs with their arms folded over their hearts, just the way Sister Roberta had instructed.

Slowly, everyone's heads began to peek out of their blankets, and Sister Aniela stepped out from behind the curtain that separated their sleeping areas. With a cheerful "A blessed morning, children," she was already fully dressed. "Time for you to wash up before chapel begins!"

Sister Aniela headed to the chapel and lit the altar candles as the other sisters processioned down the aisle to their assigned pews. The children were expected to sit in their given seats between the nuns who would guide them in proper Mass etiquette.

Elise, Colin, and Naomi had never been to an actual Catholic church. They recalled the many daily prayers they recited with the Bryk family during their last journey. The rosary, novenas, and Polish hymns returned to memory within a short time.

Max, however, had much to learn. Unfortunately, he

had no interest in the liturgy. Studying the statues and pictures of the life of Jesus was only mildly interesting. "Psst, Colin. Who's that little girl in the back with Sister Adolfina?"

I'm not going to get rapped on the knuckles again because of chatting with Max. Still, Colin couldn't resist turning around for a look and shrugged his shoulders. Sister Adolfina shot him a stern look that was enough to send a shiver down his spine. *Whew, Grandma and Papa were right about the nuns being strict.*

When morning chapel ended, everyone genuflected next to their seat and made the sign of the cross upon leaving. Colin scurried to the back of the church to test the mysterious girl. Could she see him? Colin walked back and forth in front of her, but her eyes never seemed to notice him.

In the courtyard, Colin found Sister Aniela. "Sister, who was that little girl sitting in the back with Sister Adolfina?"

"We aren't sure what to do about her with you three invisible ones. Mother Roberta thinks it's best if she doesn't know about you. Like everything else, the decision about what she should know will be made for everyone's safety."

"What about Max? Is he allowed to talk with her?" Colin asked.

"There's not much point in that. Max is an older boy, and she's a little girl. I doubt they would be friends. Besides, they aren't allowed to talk about being a Jew, even to another Jew."

Colin smiled when he realized Sister Aniela had given him the answer he wanted to know. *So, that little girl is also a Jew, and the nuns are hiding her.*

The bell at the convent gate rang, and the nuns hurried all the children inside the convent to safety. Sister Adolfina walked timidly to the gate and opened the security window.

"I'm here to see my sister." The nun inwardly cringed, knowing it was Mishka's gruff voice. A visit from the despised brother of Sister Aniela always caused some sort of trouble. Although the nuns never wanted him inside the convent walls, it seemed best to keep him calm, so she opened the door. Mishka whisked past the nun to find his sister.

Mishka and Sister Aniela couldn't have been more different in every respect. He was the very representation of the word vile, while the spirit of kindness lived in her. Mishka was filled with arrogance and self-confidence, but his sister was somewhat emotionally fragile. He was slovenly, while she was meticulous in her appearance. It was hard to believe they were related.

Sister Roberta had been alerted to Mishka's presence on the convent's grounds. Even though the children were safely tucked away from his suspicious eyes, the nun understood his cunning nature. Mishka was always finagling for an opportunity. "Why are you here, Mishka?"

Mishka snarled. "Just to see my own sister. What's wrong with that? Can't a good brother be concerned about his younger sister?"

"Monsignor told me you were banned from church grounds, and that will also be my policy at the convent."

At that moment, Sister Aniela appeared in the doorway and overheard Sister Roberta's words. "Mishka, I told you not to come here!"

"Sister Aniela, go get your brother some eggs and

bread, and then he'll be on his way."

"What illegal activities are you doing here, Sister Roberta? Are you hiding some more wounded or sick partisans?" Mishka's sinister smirk sent chills down her spine. "That's what I've heard back in town."

"God will punish you, Mishka, for your wickedness." Sister Roberta wanted to say so much more about what she had heard. About his turning in Jews to receive money from the Gestapo. About blackmailing Poles who were hiding Jews in their barns and attics. About being one of the Gestapo's prominent spies who helped the Germans oppress the Poles, who only wanted to survive under the occupation. She was wise enough to know that confronting Mishka any further would result in more problems for the convent.

Sister Aniela trembled as she handed her brother the sack with the convent's precious provisions. "Mishka, it's best if you don't come here again. Please."

Mishka muttered as he stumbled through the gate and looked back at his sister. "You think you're better than me, your own flesh and blood. Living with rosary beads in your pocket. Go pray to that invisible God of yours who left you as an orphan." Miska's voice trailed off, continuing to shout nonsense and profanities as he left the convent.

Sister Roberta secured the gate and looked back to see Sister Aniela on her knees, weeping. "I'm so sorry to have brought such wickedness into the convent. I'm so ashamed."

Sister Roberta helped the young nun up from the ground and put her hands on Sister Aniela's shoulders. "God is smiling down on you, my dear sister. We all know you are nothing like your brother. Now, go dry your tears."

Chapter Sixteen

The Gestapo

Before the sisters had time to eat breakfast, the bell at the convent sounded. Father Kurek rushed through the gate, leaving his rusty bicycle at the entrance, and ran to find Sister Roberta. He closed the door after entering her office. "There's trouble. The Gestapo is making spot inspections of all the churches and convents around Heidelager. Here, and in Debica and Mielec too."

"Are you certain of this? Are they looking for Jews or something else?" Sister Roberta asked.

"There have been at least four escapes from Pustkow and the ghetto. They're looking for the AK, Jewish refugees, both children and adults. They'll likely come here first."

"I thank you for this warning. We've already thought this out. The babies will be sedated again so they don't cry. Then we'll put them in the tent with the children under that large tree at the edge of the fields. If any of the babies cry, they might not be heard from so far away. We can't risk another incident like the one with Mishka. What if some German sees the children?"

Father Kurek blessed everyone and kissed the children before he sped away to reach the convent in Mielec. Within minutes, the roar of the Germans' trucks grew louder, and then everyone heard the pounding on the door.

"Max! Zosia! Quickly!" Sister Adolfina rushed them to the hiding places in the barn under the loose boards.

Colin and Elise whisked the babies out of their beds, and Naomi sprinted to the tent with a small bowl of sugar cubes. "I've got them!"

Sister Aniela knelt outside the tent with the last instructions for the children. "Stay until we come to tell you it's safe."

Elise hugged the nun after she blessed them and then zipped up the tent and covered the windows. "Don't worry. We'll stay in the tent until you say the coast is clear."

The Germans' loud voices echoed from the convent as the three children cradled the still, whimpering babies. Soon, the entire convent was ringed by armed soldiers.

"Where is your Mother Superior?" one of the men asked as Sister Aniela opened the gate.

She glanced up to see the terrifying image of the death's head and Nazi eagle on his cap and shuddered. Her tremoring hands clutched her crucifix, dangling from her neck, "This way."

Sister Roberta stepped into the courtyard to address the men. "I am Sister Roberta, the acting Mother Superior of this convent."

Otto Kepler wasn't the typical Arian type that populated the SS and Gestapo. His olive skin and sharp, high cheekbones seemed more Slavic. His carefully groomed, pomaded black hair contrasted with his cruel, pursed lips. Flecks of spittle flew from his mouth onto the nun's face. "We have heard reports that you've been aiding the partisans from the forests. You realize this is a crime?"

Sister Roberta winced. "There are no partisans here, nor have any come for our help." Her heart was beating so rapidly she could feel it in her ears, but she remained resolute.

"Weapons? Have you stored weapons for the partisans anywhere in the convent?"

"We are Christian women who serve the poor," Sister Roberta replied calmly. "We carry no weapons."

The two SS men threw back their heads and laughed, the sound sharp and mocking in the still air. "We are well aware that convents such as yours and the priests do more to undermine the Reich than anyone else. Tell all the sisters to wait here in the courtyard. We will interrogate them one by one in your office. In the meantime, some of our men will have a look around." The officer then clicked his heels and signaled for the others to commence the raid.

The other SS officers swarmed the convent, rummaging through drawers and closets, knocking down books, and scattering papers. Two men strolled calmly about, making notes in a journal.

The sisters in the courtyard could hear the Gestapo's shouting and scolding, but each woman's voice remained clear and calm amid their interrogation. The Germans had hoped one of the younger, more vulnerable nuns would break. Each nun left the room shaken.

The Germans surmised it would be easier to use their words as testimony against Sister Roberta's alleged actions, so her interrogation was the last. Upon entering her own office, she was disheartened to observe the Germans had rummaged through her desk and files. Otto looked so comfortable sitting in her chair as he curtly pointed to another chair. "Sit down. All you need to do is tell us the truth. Some of your little sisters gave us some insight into what has been going on here in the convent."

As Sister Roberta sat down, she desperately tried to suppress any sign of fear. Her lips trembled, and she squeezed them tightly to stop. Otto placed the fingertips of both hands together with his elbows resting on the desk's surface. His eyes examined her every movement.

"You must first know I have no admiration or respect for those who think they are heroic by giving protection to our enemies."

Sister Roberta remained silent, knowing silence was her best option if given one.

"Children are missing from the ghetto, and one of my informers there said they were taken to some convent."

"We have just received a large group of elderly nuns from L'viv and have no resources to help anyone else. You will find no children. Listen. There is only serenity in this convent day and night. Only the sisters are on these premises."

"Then you can tell me which convent has taken in these babies!"

"Sir, we have no way to communicate. No cars, no phones. Each convent has a different mission. Ours worked with the young local children, but that responsibility was taken away soon after the occupation."

"So, in your own words, your convent is useless now. That is most interesting. Regardless, my men will find evidence of your coercive activities. We will uncover them, Sister." With a dismissive wave of his hand, the commander said, "Go with the rest of your friends."

Max and Zosia sat quietly in the dark, worrying about their safety in this deadly game of hide and seek. Although they had just recently met, Zosia clutched Max as if he were her brother and squeezed him tight. The children listened intently when the men's conversation grew louder as they approached the barn. The Gestapo swung open the barn doors and thrust their bayonets into the hay. Zosia squeezed her eyes closed and prayed while Max battled the rage and heartache inside him. Zosia felt his tears drip onto her face.

Suddenly, they heard boots clumping right above them. The children overheard the men's voices, "Tie a rope around the swine's necks. Gerhard, you take a few of the hens from the coop. Leave just a few for the ladies." Their voices trailed off in laughter.

Two Germans walked to an area not far from the tent to inspect the rear of the barn. Colin, Elise, and Naomi sat frozen, clutching the sleeping babies. The soldiers, of course, saw nothing except the shocks of barley waving in the gentle breeze. The two soldiers in charge of surveying the farm's holdings walked the field's perimeter and stopped within earshot of the children. "About twenty acres of farmland, a barn in good condition, a toolshed, all kept in very usable condition, Sir." His partner replied in a matter-of-fact tone. "This convent's next on the list. Everything from this farm will soon belong to the Reich. ..."

The frantic squealing of the pigs drowned out the rest of the German officers' conversation. The three children shot knowing glances at one another, and their mouths fell open. After hearing nothing but the clucking of the hens from afar, Elise lifted the inside tent flap just an inch to observe the Gestapo walking back to the convent. "They're going to close the convent?" she whispered.

The convent grounds grew quiet after the Germans' trucks roared down the road back to Kolbuszowa. The children detected Sister Aniela's silhouette as she neared their tent. "Children, you can come out now."

The three emerged from their tent with the babies cradled in their arms. "Take the babies to the convent. I must go to Max and Zosia."

The three children carried the babies into the convent and tried to rouse them from their drug-induced sleep. "Put cool water on the faces. See if you can rouse them," Sister Roberta said.

"What if they don't wake up again?" Naomi sobbed. "I gave them those sugar cubes just like Anna told me to. Maybe I killed them."

Sister Aniela ran up and put her arms around Naomi. "Oh, no. You saved their lives. If the Gestapo heard a baby cry, we would all be killed. The babies, too. What you did is very necessary and very brave, Naomi!"

Elise lifted up the baby she had named Lucy. "See, Lucy is starting to wake up. It will be okay, Naomi."

"Stay here with the babies while I speak with the sisters," Sister Roberta said.

Colin jumped up. "Sister Aniela, tell Sister Roberta we need to tell her something important we overheard."

Elise blurted out the news. "We first heard them talking about how much land the convent owned. It seemed like they were doing an inventory of the farm. They mentioned the convent had about twenty acres of land, a barn, and a toolshed in good condition." Elise shifted in her chair and looked down. "Then he said, 'This convent is next on their list' and that the farm would soon belong to the Germans."

Sister Aniela looked down. "They took our best livestock, my mother's prize kettle, and helped themselves to the bread Sister Adolfina had just baked. I suppose we should have expected this."

"Yeah, we heard the pigs squealing when the Germans carried them from the barn," Naomi said.

"Are you certain you heard this? This is the first time we've been raided. So far, they have only made casual visits," Sister Aniela said.

"Let's just pray over this and wait until tomorrow to tell Sister Roberta. She has so many problems right now. One more day won't hurt."

Chapter Seventeen

The Cellphone Discovery

The stifling nighttime summer air mixed with the anxiety of the Germans' raid. All through the sleepless night, Naomi would reach under the pillow to feel for the phone. Although it was turned off, she still wanted to be confident it was always nearby.

Elise rolled over to see her cousin's eyes wide open. "Naomi, are you still awake?"

Naomi crawled next to Elise and whispered in her ear. "Why don't we try to find out if what we heard is true?

"We might as well, but only for maybe five minutes. We haven't really needed the cellphone so far."

The two girls discussed search terms to enter and then decided on "Trzesowka, Convent, WWII."

"Okay, here goes," Naomi said as she pressed Enter. Within seconds, several sites popped up. "I don't know which one to go to." Elise grabbed the phone. "One is about the parish in Trzesowka, and the other—oh, perfect. It says, 'Wartime Rescue of Jews in Poland by Catholic Clergy.' It shows Sister Roberta's name in the preview. Let's go there."

Colin called from his bed, "What are you guys up to?"

"Look! It's about the convent. Here's what it says,

'The work of the sisters was disrupted only by the Nazi occupiers. They were displaced in 1942 and lived for two years in Wadowice Gorne near Mielec. In Trzesowka, only Sister Adolfina Drozdz remained. The sisters returned home to Trzesowka in October 1944, where they began to reorganize, serving God and the people. It is noteworthy that in these difficult times in World War II, the sisters helped the partisans by hiding them on their premises and providing medical assistance to the injured. Risking their own lives, they helped the Jewish population. During the Nazi occupation, they hid and raised a girl, Rachel, of Jewish origin. The attitude of the then superior sister, Roberta Sutkowska, especially deserves to be highlighted.' "

"Okay, shut down the cell phone. What the Germans said is true." Colin pulled up his pants while he jumped out of bed. "Let's go wake up Sister Aniela."

Elise lit the oil lamp, and the three crept to the nun's bedroom area like they had marshmallows strapped to their shoe bottoms. Colin knocked on the door, and the nun soon cracked open the door to see their faces. Before she could say a word, the children blurted out the confirmation that the Germans planned to confiscate the convent's property. "You go to the kitchen. I'll go find Sister Roberta," Sister Aniela said. The children had never seen any of the nuns without their full habits and veils. They were surprised Sister Aniela looked rather pretty with her hair and neck exposed.

After the children explained what they had learned, Sister Roberta rubbed her forehead. "It is amazing that we can learn about the future. Help me think this through. We're halfway through 1942, so we know our convent will be closed in the next few months, although the children overheard the Germans say 'soon.' That means it could be this week or three months from now." Sister Roberta crossed her arms as she thought. "So many things to do, but the first is to find homes for the babies. We can't take them to the convent in Mielec."

Sister Roberta paced back and forth, her footsteps echoing softly against the stone floor. With each turn, she pondered the consequences, the ripple effects her choice would have on the people she cared for, and the path their lives would take.

"Sister Aniela, you'll need to take the babies by cart to find homes for them as soon as possible."

"I can't manage the cart and babies by myself. Will the children be able to come with me?" Sister Aniela asked.

The three glanced at one another, and their collective beaming faces needed no explanation.

Naomi bounced up and down and delivered their reply. "Sister Aniela, you bet we're coming with you!"

Chapter Eighteen

Home Army Partisans

"I can see the convent, Alex. Just…try to keep going." Józef's voice was low but urgent as the two partisans hugged the edge of the road, melting into the shadows beneath the trees. His arm was locked around his friend's waist, but Alex's weight dragged with every step.

They were almost there, almost safe, yet Józef could feel Alex slipping away.

Alex sagged to the ground behind a thick clump of bushes. "I…can't go…any farther." His voice was barely more than a rasp.

"I'll get help." Józef scanned the road, his eyes darting for any sign of movement. "Just stay alive. You hear me? Stay alive."

Without another word, the tall, gangly Home Army partisan burst from the cover of the trees. His boots pounded the dirt as he crossed the road, each stride fueled by desperation. In moments, he was at the convent gates, hammering the bell.

Inside, Sister Roberta paused. No rumble of German trucks, no sharp voices outside. This visitor was in trouble. She opened the window.

"Sister, my friend's been wounded. He needs help, now," Józef pleaded, his breath ragged.

The nun wasted no time. She threw open the door and ushered him inside.

"He's in the woods, just beyond the road," Józef said quickly. "Is there anyone here strong enough to help carry him?"

Sister Roberta pressed a hand to her mouth, thinking. Then her eyes lit with a decision. "Sister Aniela, find Colin."

Colin hurried to the courtyard and then froze. "Uncle Józef!" His eyes grew the size of saucers as he bolted to embrace his great-uncle.

At first startled, Józef smiled widely when he recognized the young man. "You must be Colin. Anna told me the whole story. That you had returned, but she wouldn't tell me where you were."

"Always the good partisan. Not revealing anything that might cause us harm to a member of her cell." Colin exclaimed.

After the nun explained the pressing need, Colin followed Józef into the woods. Józef described his fellow partisan's injury and the need for extreme discretion. Just as they left the convent gate, Naomi raced to catch up with her Girl Scout backpack on her shoulders. "I'm coming too! I have my first aid kit!"

Colin was just about to shoo her back to the convent, but then remembered. Naomi and her backpack would be invisible. "Are you really ready to see blood, Naomi?"

"Uh, I think so…" Naomi sputtered, but then felt a rush of adrenaline to keep going. "Hey, I have my Girl Scout's first aid badge to prove it. I'm ready!"

The three arrived just minutes later to find their friend seemingly unconscious. Józef patted Alex on the leg to rouse him, knowing he had a better chance of survival if he stayed alert.

"Naomi, is there gauze and a pin in your kit? Alex is losing blood from the wound on the back of his leg. Let's get it wrapped."

Naomi shuddered as she helped to wrap the wound tightly. "Here's two clips to keep it tight."

"You're a pro! A real nurse!" Józef exclaimed.

"I practiced on my stuffed animals!" Naomi said.

Alex smiled at the sweetness of her efforts and whispered, "Thank you, Nurse Naomi."

The two men lifted Alex to cradle him in their arms. "Got him secure?" Józef asked.

Alex moaned and began to examine the other person who had come to his aid. His eyes strained to examine the young teen, who was probably taller than he was. "I know you, but I can't remember from where." At that point, nothing made sense, so Alex kept his gaze on the forward path through the trees. "The sisters must have sent two angels to help me. Right, Józef?"

Józef wanted to laugh at this peculiar event, but was surprised that Alex could see Colin and Naomi. "Sort of. They're angels from America. I'll explain later."

"What?" Alex said groggily. "The Americans have arrived? I had no idea they were so close to Poland!"

The sisters were at the gate to guide the partisans into the convent. Elise stood horrified at the sight of the soldier, bloodied and in obvious pain, as Colin and Josef carried Alex into the courtyard.

Elise ran to assist Naomi, who proudly walked behind the men. "That soldier helping is Józef, your great-uncle, Naomi. He's the one who gave me the doll," Elise said. "Józef's about the nicest person I've ever met."

"This way. Into the sleeping area." Sister Roberta guided them to her room. "Józef, I see the leg wound. Are there other injuries?"

"A bullet went clear through his leg. He's lost quite a bit of blood. I wasn't able to examine him any more than that."

After carefully cutting away the fabric of Alex's trousers, Sister Roberta flushed out both wounds with boiled water cooled to a tolerable temperature. She would have preferred using carbolic acid but that had been gone from the convent's meager supplies for over a year. She asked Sister Aniela to fetch her herbal medicine kit. Like many other nuns in occupied Poland who had trained as nurses before the war, she was forced to rely on folk remedies and whatever scraps of bandaging the convent could spare.

Alex clenched his teeth when she dabbed a greenish extract of comfrey over the entry and exit wounds, a peasant remedy believed to draw out infection. With no proper antiseptic, she sprinkled a pinch of burnt sugar into the wound to discourage the growth of bacteria, then laid thin paper salvaged from an old newspaper beneath the gauze to absorb blood and prevent the cloth from sticking.

She wrapped the leg tightly, layer upon layer, securing it with strips of clean cotton cut from worn-out bedsheets. "Even though it is hot outside, keep him warm. He's lost a dangerous amount of blood," she said, tucking a blanket around his shivering body. She then motioned for Józef to step outside the room.

"Colin, you stay with Alex," Józef said.

Colin wanted to remind them that he wasn't a doctor or nurse but sat dutifully at the wounded soldier's bedside. Alex's eyes fluttered as he opened them to see Colin inspecting the newly bloodied linen wrappings on his leg. "You're the strong guy who carried me in here."

Colin shook his head and nodded. He then studied Alex's cleaned-up face. "I think I met you when I was here before. Yeah. We met with a group of partisans."

Alex shook his head wearily. "I don't remember that."

Colin smiled, knowing that Alex wasn't strong enough for an explanation of the future. "I'll explain it later." He remembered how Alex had told him what life was like as a partisan living in the forests surrounding the SS Camp. Colin also recalled that Alex was to be Anna's fiancé, but the Russians captured him when the Germans had to flee the area. After the war, he was a doomed soldier and was never seen again. Alex was another person who shouldn't be told his future.

Colin went into the hallway just as Sister Roberta was explaining the convent's problems to Józef. "We've been informed the convent will be closing sometime in the future. Tomorrow? Three months from now? Who knows?"

Józef's forehead wrinkled. "Then Alex will need to be moved. I've nowhere safe to take him."

"The Gestapo raided us just yesterday." Sister Roberta put her hand to her mouth and gazed upward as she considered the possibilities. "We've some infants here that will need to be placed in homes. Very soon. They were kept in the children's tent during the Germans' inspection. That tent makes everything inside invisible, so that's where we will keep Alex when he is out of danger."

"Very soon, I hope," Józef said.

Colin stepped forward. "Józef, come out back, and I'll show you. It wasn't easy hiding those babies!" Colin then hesitated. "Is that all right, Sister?"

Sister Roberta nodded gratefully, overwhelmed with so many needs. "I must think of how to get the babies and Max and Zosia into a safer place. We can't burden the convent in Mielec with all these sisters and so many Jewish children to hide."

Chapter Nineteen

The Villagers

Several days later, Sister Roberta and Josef were ready to move on with their well-thought-out plans. Now, in mid-July, the villagers' and Jews' situation in the areas surrounding Camp Heidelager had deteriorated even further. The Gestapo conducted a massive roundup of the Jews in nearby Radomysl. It was just a few miles from the convent in Mielec to which the nuns of the Sisters of St. Joseph would soon flee.

The Jews of the Kolbuszowa ghetto who could work were sent to the ghetto in Debica. Unfortunately, the old, young, and infirm met an early death in the Jewish cemeteries' deep pits. Stories of the Germans' revenge against any Pole who assisted the Jews left the sisters concerned about their next actions at the convent. Any missteps might result in the tragic death of the innocent as the Germans implemented collective revenge. Even if a person was not directly involved in helping a Jew, the Gestapo demanded that the entire community experience their wrath. The terror evolved to the point of burning entire Polish villages and shooting ten randomly chosen Poles.

Józef spent most nights with the partisans hidden in the nearby forests, returning to sleep in the barn by day with his rifle, boots, and satchel always within arm's reach. If the Gestapo paid another visit to the convent, he could be gone in seconds. When German vehicles approached, their deafening roar shattered the convent's usual tranquility, a jarring reminder of danger pressing at its gates.

Sister Roberta pondered how to close down the convent covertly without signaling the Germans that the sisters knew of their plans. After Father Kurek and Monsignor Dunajecki arrived from Kolbuszowa, she gathered Sister Aniela, Sister Adolfina, the three children, and Józef to join them in the dining hall.

"Starting early tomorrow morning, Sister Aniela will work with Elise and Naomi to find homes for the babies in the areas north of Heidelager. We'll ask the parishes to keep our personal items and records. Colin will stay at the convent to help Alex in case the Germans arrive. The harvest is just starting to come in, so the sisters will work in the fields. The officials keep such close records, and they know how much grain and produce we will have. There's no use in trying to deceive them. That would only result in severe punishment for the convent."

Everyone nodded in agreement except the three children. They gave a knowing glance to one another, and then Elise spoke up. "Everything sounds like the right thing to do, except that would mean the three of us would be separated. What if that's the moment meant for us to return home?"

Colin added, "We promised each other we wouldn't separate."

Father Kurek nodded. "Can I stay with Alex so Colin can travel with the girls?"

A flicker of regret crossed Sister Roberta's face.

How could she have overlooked something so important? "I apologize to you, children. I forgot that you needed to stay together, but I'm not aware of your reason."

"We aren't sure, but when we were here before, we were transported back to our real homes in the future when my cellphone battery died. We can't chance leaving one of us behind."

"I understand the importance now. Of course, you must stay together," Sister Roberta said.

"What about Max and Zosia? Where will they go?" Elise asked.

"Zosia has every feature of a Pole and is a girl, so she will stay with us at the Mielec convent. Max will stay with Andrzej and Zeffie, your relatives, in Radomysl Wielki."

The cooling rains falling all night were a welcome relief. Everyone at the convent was preparing for the babies' departure. Józef attached the horse to the cart while the three cousins brought out the babies.

Sister Aniela was amazed at how the two young girls had mastered caring for babies, even the colicky one they nicknamed Stashu. "Naomi, here's the bag with the sugar cubes, just in case you might need them."

"You're taking only these three babies." Sister Roberta handed Elise a piece of paper. "Finding homes for them won't be easy, but here's a list of kind Poles from the villages of Cmolas and Majdan who may take the babies. The house numbers are right there also."

Colin leaped with ease onto the bench with Sister Aniela. She leaned over to whisper. "Are you getting tired of being a babysitter?"

"A little," Colin smirked. "During our first trip,

Elise and I worked with the partisans and almost never saw a Nazi. We have never witnessed firsthand how horrible they are. Now, I see these Germans are really despicable."

Elise called out, "Three babies? Check! Cloaks of invisibility? Check!"

"What about my Girl Scout backpack and cellphone? Check! Check!" Naomi half-laughed.

"How about if I man the reins today?" Colin asked.

"That would be just fine until someone spots our horse cart driven by an invisible person." Sister Aniela laughed at the possible scene of a forester spotting them. "I'd be asked about my magic horse-driving tricks till the day I die."

Colin pleaded, "Just for a little while until we see someone up ahead? Then, I'll transfer the reins." Sister Aniela smiled as she put Colin in charge.

The nun and children meandered down the back roads in the forests of Sandomierz, the so-called "roads" little more than wide dirt paths, hemmed in by towering pines and tangled undergrowth. The steady, rhythmic beat of the horse's hooves seemed to echo their thoughts, each thud a reminder of the world they had left behind.

Colin stared at the swaying leather reins and thought about all the games and practices he was missing—how the smell of fresh-cut grass at the ballfield was nothing like the earthy scent of the Polish woods, and how his teammates would be running drills without him. Elise's mind wandered to the bright lights of her dance studio and the feel of smooth wooden floors beneath her feet, to the warm applause after her performances in musicals— sounds so far removed from the creak of the cart wheels and the distant call of a cuckoo. Naomi pictured her parents' smiling faces and the gentle hum of cicadas during summer vacations at her grandparents' house in Ohio, where the air was thick with the aroma of freshly baked pies and mown lawns.

But shadowing all those warm memories was the same unspoken thought. What if they never returned? What if this strange and dangerous adventure ended differently than the last? The question settled over them like an unwelcome passenger in the cart, heavy and silent.

The squirrels scampered into the woods with their treasures when they saw the sojourners' cart approaching. Sister Aniela pointed to the right at a fork in the road. "The first house should be down this road if my memory serves me. I'm not very familiar with these parts."

After passing two abandoned homes, a house built of unhewn trees perched in a clearing came into view. "That's the Szumierz's house."

The door and white framed windows were open, and Lucjan was piling firewood against the side of his home. He glanced up and recognized the young nun. Lucjan sprinted to open the gate. "Sister Aniela! It's been months since I last saw you!"

"Praise be our Lord. How good to see you are well."

"Zofia is visiting with her mother this morning. She will be so sorry to have missed your visit."

Sister Aniela turned to the children and asked them to bring Bieta, one of the infants, from the wagon. "Lucjan, it's become very dangerous at the convent, and what you are about to witness is truly a miracle. Children from the future are with me. We sisters consider them to be angels of the Lord. One of them is holding a baby that needs a home."

Lucjan's eyes lit up when he saw a baby seemingly floating in midair. He stepped backward and stumbled on the front step. "Lord Jesus, what am I seeing? Come. Bring the invisible children and baby into the house."

Naomi cradled Bieta, who always stayed calm, while Sister Aniela showed Lucjan the birth record Monsignor Dunajecki had provided.

Elise and Colin inspected the large single-room wooden house. Elise inhaled the fragrance of the freshly baked bread sitting on the nearby counter. "Colin, this looks so much like Jadwiga's house. Just one space for living, a loft, a storage area, and a packed clay floor." Along the walls were two beds, and in the corner were cast iron pots sitting on a huge two-chambered ceramic stove.

Naomi transferred the baby to Sister Aniela and joined her cousins. She toured the room and admired the blue chest painted with roosters and flowers. "Is that what Jadwiga's house looked like?"

"Pretty much. We didn't get to see other people's homes, only hers. It had the same things as this one." Elise replied.

"They don't have many things, do they?" Naomi observed. She wasn't sure if that was ultimately a good thing or not. "Not like us back home."

Under the solemn religious artwork adorning the walls was an ivory beeswax candle. "Look, a gromnica! I wonder if we could light this and go back home?" Naomi asked. A rush of emotions overcame the youngest cousin, who had tried hard to suppress missing her parents and family.

Lucjan reached out his arms to take little Bieta.

"Yes, of course, Zofia and I will take in the infant. How could we say no when angels from the Lord bring the baby to us?"

Sister Aniela handed Lucjan a bag with a bottle and some supplies. "Someone from Kolbuszowa will bring the revised birth record for you soon. It will have your names on it."

"Bieta is certainly a beautiful child. The only problem is my wife. She may think I was drinking or seeing things when I tell her about the invisible angels and how I saw a baby floating in midair," Lucjan laughed.

"Assure Zofia that a sister from our convent will come to visit soon and will reassure her. Maybe the children will still be with us, and they can also come."

After leaving Lucjan's home, the four continued down the winding roads on their mission to find homes for the two others. Sister Aniela pulled back on the reins to stop at a fork in the road. Her face flushed, and she shook her head. "Oh, dear. I think we're lost. I have no idea how to get to the next house."

"Why don't we go back and ask that nice man, Lucjan?" Naomi asked.

"No, that would break our promise to keep the other villagers' identities safe," Colin said. "Hey, how about we try using an online map?"

"It's worth a try," Elise said.

Naomi retrieved her phone from her backpack and gave it to Colin. "I don't know how to use maps."

"Sister Aniela, tell me their address as if you are going to send them a letter."

The nun looked up to visualize how it should be stated. "How about 460 Cmolas, Poland."

"It worked, I think…" Colin showed the map to Sister Aniela, who noted that the house was only a short ride from their location.

"Angels with machines to guide us." Sister Aniela said. "I wasn't telling a lie when I told Lucjan you were angels. How else can we explain what you are doing for us?"

At the next stop, the travelers initially met just a bit of resistance. After explaining the story, the family agreed with the request. When the children showed their actions, they knew the appeal must have come from God's heart. Jakub and Francisca were pleased to accept the colicky Stashu.

Colin, Elise, and Naomi each had a special place in their heart for a specific baby. Now it was Elise's turn to release baby Petronella to another kind family. "Naomi, can we take a picture of her with your cellphone? We need some photos to document our adventure."

Naomi turned her cell phone back on and took photos of everyone, including the house and horse.

Colin grabbed the phone to inspect the charge. "Hey, you're down to 60% now. You do know your battery drains even if it isn't turned on, right?"

As they successfully left baby Petronella at the last home, the children collapsed on the hay wagon for the ride home. They saw another cart coming from the other direction when they were about five miles from the convent. "Children, bury yourselves as much as possible."

The children burrowed onto their stomachs under the hay and tried to remain as still as possible. As the cart approached, Sister Aniela cringed when she saw it was her brother, Mishka.

Mishka stumbled as he jumped off his wagon. "Sister! Where are you going? I was just at the convent to see you."

"What is it that you want, Mishka?"

"Can't a brother come to see his only sister?"

"We both know that you don't come just to visit."

Mishka approached the cart. "You know I'm not doing so well right now with my bad leg. Are there any foods you have hidden in here in the wagon?"

Mishka began to rustle through the hay and touched Colin's shirt. "What's this under here?" He then removed enough hay to discover the children.

Sister Aniela screamed, "These are Polish children. Leave them alone."

"Aren't these the ones I saw with Father Kurek? They were supposed to go to meet some relative!" Mishka bellowed, his voice as coarse as gravel. His eyes, small and calculating, darted between the children and Sister Aniela.

"Our uncle was killed on the way. We never met up with him," Colin blurted before he could stop himself.

"Colin, Mishka doesn't deserve to know. We need to get back to the convent," Sister Aniela said sharply. She knew better than most that Mishka thrived on other people's misfortunes. Her brother was infamous in the area—mean-spirited, perpetually reeking of vodka, and known to cheat neighbors out of whatever he could.

"I need about a hundred zlotys to keep quiet about this, now that I know you and the sisters are hiding children. I'll be by to visit you soon, sister." His smirk revealed several yellowed teeth, and the greed in his eyes left no doubt he would follow through.

Sister Aniela didn't wait for Mishka to step back from the cart. She snapped the reins, and as the horse surged forward, the wheel rolled squarely over his foot. A stream of vulgarities burst from his foul mouth, words so filthy even the woods seemed to recoil from the sound.

When they arrived back at the convent, Sister Aniela bolted to find Sister Roberta to tell her about the encounter with Mishka.

"Sister Aniela, don't blame yourself. We have many like Mishka who are the dregs of society." Sister Roberta rubbed the back of her neck and blew out a deep breath. "Even though the Germans can't see the children, we don't want Mishka to see them again either."

"I'm sure he'll be back."

"Let me handle him when he does. You aren't to answer the bell for a while for your own safety. And don't worry about the children. We have a new plan for them. Now that we've found homes for the babies, we only need to worry about Max and Zosia."

Sister Roberta called for the children to meet in the office with her. To their surprise, Anna Grabiec was already there. The girls ran up to embrace her.

Although excited to see Anna, Colin wondered if it was time for them to go back home. Although they had been helpful in the rescues, their presence created a considerable problem with Mishka's suspicions. "Sister Roberta, maybe it's time for us to gather around the cell phone and make it power down."

Elise couldn't shake the memory of Mishka's evil presence. "I'm sorry we're causing so many problems, Sister Roberta."

"Oh, no. Children. Look at what just happened with

the babies you helped. Those people who took in the babies sensed God's supernatural power. He was asking them to accept a baby. They took them even though it might put their entire family in danger. Sister Roberta's eyes misted. "The sisters and everyone who has met you three truly believe God has sent you."

"But, what if Mishka comes back to the convent? What if he talks to the Gestapo, and they come back?" Colin asked.

"Those are real possibilities, but now Anna needs your help," Sister Roberta replied.

The children sat at the edge of their seats, excited that a new adventure might be ahead of them. Elise could hardly wait to work with Anna again.

Anna sat at the table with her hands folded. "Children, there's a group of people in Warsaw who are rescuing babies from the ghetto in that city. They're asking for help from all the convents in the General Government, even those like this one that are far away. We think you can be very helpful in this operation. What do you think about traveling to Radom with me and Father Kurek?"

Although the children were discouraged just a minute ago, Anna's news was like fireworks exploding in their chests. Their beaming faces revealed the answer.

Anna was as excited as the children about their next whirlwind adventure. "This one is going to be pretty complicated. Father Kurek and I will accompany you on the train to meet up for the drop in a town south of Warsaw, and then we will take the train back to Debica. There, we will travel by horse cart to the home of a very important woman who will pay people to take the babies into their home.

Sister Roberta chimed in. "Elise and Naomi, have you ever met a countess?"

"A princess? Like kings and queens?" Naomi's raised eyebrows and clenched teeth revealed her excitement at the prospect of meeting a real, live princess. She imagined a beautiful girl in a blue satin gown, but this princess was the forty-three-year-old Helena Jabłonowska. The countess was known for her influence and for funding the partisans in the forest. Even the Germans had a healthy respect for this noble woman.

Anna smiled widely at Naomi's excitement but had to admit she was also in awe of this woman. "Some people refer to her as a princess, but more correctly, she is called Countess. Helena was born into a royal household but now dedicates her life to Poland's freedom and the care of the poor. It is Helena who is paying for our expenses so we can ride in a first-class train car with no one else."

"I've never been on a train before. Not a real one. Is this mission as risky as the others?" Colin asked. This adventure seemed to have all the intrigue, like he did working with the Home Army last time.

"Nothing is truly safe, but if you are Polish and have the proper documents, there should be no problem. I take the train to church almost every week." Anna fanned herself with a thin book. "There will be three babies, one for each of you to hide in your special covers, and two other Jewish children. That's all we know. The name of the contact is Irena Sendler. She will meet us at the train station."

Chapter Twenty

Train to Radom

The blare of the train whistle signaled it would soon arrive at the station. Father Kurek patted the falsified documents of himself and the children in the inside pocket of his jacket. He rather liked wearing such fine clothing. Although it fit him well, the borrowed suit seemed strange. It had been years since the priest had worn non-clerical clothing in public. That he was to pose as Anna's husband, traveling with a nephew and two nieces, was more than an intriguing adventure. However, any misstep meant he would be shot or sent to a concentration camp after days of torture.

Monsignor Dunajecki sat perched beside his young associate on a wooden bench and smirked. "Jan, how does it feel knowing you will be traveling like a rich man? First-class tickets and enough money for fine food." After guiding the horse to bring everyone to the rail station of this more distant town, the monsignor would now have to say goodbye to the courageous group of rescuers.

Anna, always the planner, gathered the group in a circle. "We need to have our stories straight. On our way to Radom, you, Colin, are our nephew, and Elise and Naomi are our two nieces. You are traveling to visit your grandmother in Lublin. On the way back, we will tell people you are visiting your grandparents in Debica. Don't worry if anyone sees you because you all look like Polish children, and you know your prayers. The biggest concern is too much talking."

"What if we need to talk to you?" Elise asked.

"Only if absolutely necessary. People who talk too much are looked at suspiciously. And don't stare at other people. That makes everyone uncomfortable. Keep your head down and read the books you brought."

Father Kurek wished to ease their minds. "Today will be quite exciting for you, I think. You will see what life is like in a Polish city. You've only experienced life in the villages thus far."

The five walked to the train station, which was nothing more than a drab cement building with a wooden platform. Except for the Nazi flag, the station was like a black-and-white movie with no color. Father Kurek took Colin by the arm. "The ticket master has returned. Let's go purchase our tickets."

Two German guards, distracted by their own conversation, walked past them. Colin's throat went dry, and he wiped both palms on his pants.

"You're nervous because you are out in the open with so many people and Germans parading about," Father Kurek said. "Just remember this is not a day for second-guessing or worrying. Keep your focus, and our mission will be successful."

A harsh, metallic shriek heralded the arrival of the northbound train. The conductor took their tickets, inspected their documents, and then escorted them to their car. His stern demeanor quickly turned gracious when he recognized them as fellow Poles, rather influential or wealthy ones at that. Anna realized the benefit of their nicely tailored suits and designer clothing for the children. Helena Jabłonowska had taken care of every detail.

Noting the conductor's eyes never glanced at the children, Father Kurek and Anna didn't offer the children's ID. After offering his assistance if needed, he slid the door closed and left them alone.

Despite being first-class, the seats' slightly corroded iron and worn upholstery spoke of better days. Naomi and Elise insisted on sitting by Anna's window while Father Kurek hunkered down next to Colin. "So, you're my uncle. Are you Uncle Jan?"

Father Kurek chuckled. "Jan Grabiec from Kolbuszowa, at your service."

Anna snickered, not realizing the monsignor had given the priest her last name. "So, you have taken my last name now that we are married?" Jokes about their situation ran through her mind, but it wouldn't be proper to say them out loud, especially in front of the children.

Naomi was mesmerized by the entire adventure, the clothing, the inside of a steam train, and that Father Kurek and Maria were now pretending to be married. "You two really aren't married, are you?"

Elise snickered and then whispered, "No, they're just pretending like we are pretending to be their nieces."

The train jerked forward as the brakes were released and inched onward at an excruciatingly slow pace. The engine whined and groaned as it began to pick up speed. The priest became engrossed in some old Polish novel while Anna used the time to close her eyes. Each stop along the way brought a rush of anxiety, with the children wondering if that station was theirs. Naomi's fingernails were almost bitten down to the nub.

After four hours, the conductor knocked on the window before entering. "Your stop is next. It was a pleasure to have you onboard."

Radom's railway station was a vast cavity with hordes of travelers, sellers, and locals. Beggars attempting to blend into the masses made their way to Father Kurek. He gave each a small coin, resisting his typical response to bless the unfortunate.

The street from the station was narrow and muddy, and the air was impregnated with competing odors. The group trekked past small shops selling baked goods and meats, but Father Kurek recognized these as German stores, which were, of course, off-limits. The smell of onions and fried foods guided them past a stand selling prepared food for travelers.

Anna whispered, "There's Dluga Street. We turn right. The apartment is not far." As they gazed down Dluga, the children marveled at the three and four-story apartments lining the tidy street. Each building seemed to have windows of different sizes on each floor. Every grim-faced person they passed peered straight ahead. The children slowed to glance through an elegant restaurant's window. The diners smiled and chattered as they sipped their steaming cups of coffee and tea.

"This is it." Anna turned into the entrance, walked up the steps leading into the building, and signaled the others to follow. Elise noted the numbers on the mailboxes in the small, stuffy hallway. The adults trudged up the creaky wooden stairs to the fourth floor while the children bounded up the steps, displaying the energy of youth.

Anna knocked on the door with the number 429 in a gold metal frame and heard the peephole click. Slightly opening the door with a heavy chain still attached to the doorframe, a woman's voice said, "Yes?"

"I'm looking for Kitty," Anna replied.

"And you are?"

"Teacher."

Without a word, she opened the door and rushed them inside. Before closing the door, she inspected the hallways to see if other residents had witnessed her guests. "I'm Kitty, and these two are Rex and Betty. Jolanta hasn't yet arrived from Warsaw. You will stay with us until she comes. Perhaps on tomorrow's train."

Kitty was a rather stylish woman with an elegant upswept hairdo. She seemed tightly wound, but that was typical all over occupied Poland. No one in WWII Poland immediately let down their guard, even after a proper introduction. "We have cots in the attic for tonight."

"There's one matter that needs the utmost secrecy," Father Kurek said. "You may find it difficult to believe, but I assure you the situation is real."

Kitty's grin was one earned through wartime experiences. She smiled and said, "We've learned to believe anything is possible in Poland during the occupation."

"Standing right next to me are three children from the future. You can't see them because only those who are related are able to see or hear them." Father Kurek never grew weary of telling the children's story to those he could trust. "Children, go sit at the table."

The three pulled out the chairs, sat, and then pushed themselves closer to the table. They folded the boldly patterned tablecloth and set it to the side. Naomi performed an additional illusion by lifting the candle holders up and down.

The three Poles all sat back in their chairs, not knowing what they had seen or what they should say.

Father Kurek grinned. "The two eldest have experience as partisans from past missions, and the youngest is still in training." Naomi harumphed.

Anna quickly came to Naomi's defense. "Naomi is extraordinary, though, as she is the one who has been trained as a Girl Guide and brought her backpack and communication device."

"Realize the children can see and hear you. Anna and I can see and hear them because we are their blood relatives. It's complicated."

Naomi couldn't take her eyes off Kitty, who seemed quite sophisticated to her. "Could you ask Kitty if she knows anything about the Girl Guides?"

"Kitty, Naomi wonders if you might have been a Girl Guide?" Anna asked.

"Girl Guides! Both Betty and I were guides. Being a guide was the best decision I ever made. The guide organization prepared many partisans for what we are doing now. From them, we learned more than jamboree camp songs. Defending our homeland from possible attacks from our evil neighbors has always been our purpose. Don't get me wrong, though. I had a wonderful time as a Girl Guide."

Everyone could sense the women's warm memories of the Guides as Kitty continued. "When the occupation began, the Boy and Girl Scouts, we call them Guides in Poland, became the country's littlest army. Guides were known to be trustworthy and generous. We took an oath to be a friend to anyone who asked for help or friendship."

Anna couldn't resist sharing memories of her scouting years. "Oh, how I loved my uniform. All crisp with the fleur-de-lis badge. I thought I was very impressive marching just like the Boy Scouts and showing off my first aid skills."

"Most of us learned to shoot rifles, bows, and arrows. When the Polish army went underground, they quickly recognized any young woman who was a Girl Guide to be a valuable resource." Betty said.

Kitty continued. "The Germans hold those of us who were Guides with great suspicion of being a partisan, so now we refer to our ranks as 'The Clover Union.' Polish doctors and nurses trust those of us who have been trained by the Red Cross. They provide us packages with medications to take to the front for injured partisan soldiers."

After learning their importance, Elise now envied her cousin Naomi's role as a Girl Guide. She remembered Anna had made her an honorary guide during her previous trip and even presented her with a Guide badge. It just didn't seem as important as deciding to be a scout.

Betty continued, "Besides our activities in Zegota to help the Jews, the young women from the Clover Union act as couriers and decoders for the AK. Many continue to run underground schools since most education in Poland has been outlawed. We typically don't get into battle in the forested areas, but some Guides do reconnaissance and sabotage on railways."

"We don't just sit home and knit scarves for the soldiers like Guides in some other parts of Europe. Many female Guides in the occupied countries are involved in dangerous activities. Most have taken the AK oath,"

Kitty said.

Father Kurek was warmed by the bravery of these three patriots, "Great, heroic acts often come from humble beginnings. Colin, do you realize you are in the presence of five Girl Guides, all in this room?"

Colin was visibly impressed and somewhat overwhelmed by the female camaraderie. "Sounds like they do lots more than most soldiers."

Kitty smiled when Maria reported Colin's comment to her and then jumped to her feet. "I'll prepare something for everyone to eat."

"Could we go to the restaurant below to eat?" Colin asked.

"Maybe I could fetch some food and bring it up here," Anna replied.

"The restaurant?" Kitty replied. "Do you want to eat there? No! You eat here!" Anna understood that proper Polish hospitality meant you never allowed guests to eat at a restaurant. Meals were prepared and eaten at home.

Father Kurek took off his hat. "I know the children would like to eat at a real Polish restaurant. They were drooling as we walked past the bakeries and restaurants. But, of course, they can't risk being seen, so that is impossible."

Kitty decided to come to the rescue. "Maybe we can do the next best thing. I work alone at the restaurant in the overnight hours, cleaning and preparing the food for the next day." Once a high-level clerk at a bank, Kitty was typical of the once-prosperous Poles who experienced job demotions and a decline in status during the war. Rex was a mechanical engineer but now worked as a mechanic for a boiler company.

"There's almost always food left for us to sell on the

black market. No one will miss a few croissants or sausages. Rex, come with me, and we'll bring up some food for our guests. The children can imagine that our apartment is a restaurant."

While Kitty and Rex went to fetch the food, the children wandered about the apartment. They had only seen the more humble homes in the villages. With its wooden floors, electricity, and running water, the flat seemed luxurious in comparison. The sturdy blueish-green upholstered sofa and chairs seemed like they were built to last forever. Obviously, its residents were well-educated since the desk had a brass lamp, a stack of letters, and an inkwell for writing.

"You'll sleep in the attic. It is very safe there because of this." Rex pointed to a bookcase filled with books, stacks of newspapers, and photos. He pulled out a few books and pulled a steel lever that allowed him to push the door. As it rotated, a steep staircase appeared.

Not one easily impressed, Colin's eyes widened. "This is so cool! A hidden staircase!"

Father Kurek agreed, and the group proceeded up the mysterious stairway. "We'll leave the door open unless the Gestapo shows up."

"And how often does that happen?" Anna asked.

"The Gestapo visits some apartment on this street every few days. We sometimes hear sporadic gunfire, but so far, we haven't been bothered."

Rex turned on the ceiling light fixture in the dimly lit room. Eight cots were neatly made up with white linens on top of thin goose feather mattresses. They seemed like crisply outfitted soldiers, all lined up on the wall like a school dormitory. "The ladies will sleep on this side. I'll bring up a room divider so you are all comfortable."

Naomi looked around the sparsely furnished attic for a bathroom and then whispered to Anna about the urgency.

Anna whispered back, "I think we all have that question. Rex, is the bathroom available for our use?"

"Of course, forgive me. I should have shown you before we came up here." Rex guided them back down the stairs and left the bookcase open a crack. "In here."

Fortunately, the chipped white porcelain fixtures were in working condition, although the sink was marred with rust stains. Naomi inspected the green-painted wooden cabinet holding all sorts of jars, bottles, and grooming and shaving supplies. She washed her hands with the thin bar of orange soap and used one of the mismatched towels hanging from wooden knobs. Grateful she didn't have to use an outhouse, Naomi realized life was very different in Polish cities than in the villages.

The fragrance of onions and savory mushrooms wafted through the air, announcing dinner. "Here we are! Beet soup, mushroom soup, cabbage and noodles, bread, golabki, and for the children, plum kuchen!"

After a satisfying meal, Anna suggested the children wash up before retiring to their sleeping quarters. The five then trudged up the stairs, all appreciating the most substantial feast they'd had in ages.

The distant clanging of a trolley from the street outside and the muted voices of passersby wafted through the window. They all wanted nothing more than to lie down and be enveloped by the melodiousness of silence.

The attic room itself was as quiet as an owl

whooshing to its prey. Anna smiled at Father Kurek and closed her eyes. He stared at her and realized this was the first time he had ever slept in the same room with a female who wasn't family. Father Kurek breathed a heavy, thoughtful sigh. This is not the way my life was supposed to go. How in the world did a priest end up on this mission? He pondered his first year as a pastor when the war broke out, barely knowing the names of most of his people. How different would his life have been if he had not chosen the priesthood? Imagining himself as the leader of a family like this, Father Kurek recognized the burden of responsibility of being the patriarch. Perhaps the priesthood was a more suitable challenge.

Chapter Twenty-One

A Gestapo Raid

At first, it was the deafening roar of motors, the familiar clicking heels of the German soldiers' boots, and doors slamming. Then, fists pounding on a door. Everyone in the attic startled and jumped out of bed. Father Kurek signaled them to be silent and tiptoed to peek out the window. "Gestapo! They're across the street." The flickering streetlight allowed the petrified priest to witness five Gestapo officers entering the apartment. He braced for what he knew would surely come next. Within minutes, sounds of destruction resonated in the nighttime air. Then gunshots echoed. Everyone froze as each blast seemed to happen in slow motion. Screams. Shouting. Cars followed by ambulances and police wagons later carried the dead or wounded away.

"Just like all the other raids and assaults I've seen over the past several years." Father Kurek solemnly walked back to his bed. "I think we're safe now, but children, remember this night when you return to your lives back in America. This is what happens when a country like Germany is misled by wickedness and is ruled by evil. We Poles have lost our precious freedom, and so many of us have lost our lives."

Elise cradled her tearing young cousin in her arms.

She softly whispered, "I bet you miss your mom and dad. Colin and I miss our parents, too." The weight of the moment pressed heavily upon them as they struggled to comprehend the harrowing reality that had unfolded before their eyes. They had all just witnessed a Gestapo raid.

As the echoes of the raid gradually faded into silence, Colin recognized the danger they were all in. He stared at his cell phone, now at a twenty percent charge. Should he just keep it on and then run to embrace the girls when it was about to lose power? Was it the right thing to subject his sister and cousin to the horrors of a war that wasn't really theirs?

Anna sat cross-legged on the wooden floor beside the girls' cots, gently smoothing their hair as if to quiet both their thoughts and her own. Naomi's eyes stayed wide open, her mind far from sleep, turning over the thought that soon she would be meeting the real Irena Sendler.

At the same time, Father Kurek prayed for the protection of this unusual partisan cell here in the attic. "Now, let's try to be thankful that we are alive and that God is using us to help save some of His Chosen Ones. Lord, calm our minds."

Only complete exhaustion could explain how the five managed to get any sleep, but they all slept until daybreak. When they awoke, Anna brushed each girl's hair and then placed a huge bow at the top of their heads. "There, now you look like proper upper-crust Polish children." She patted each one on the head. "Look at what Sister Roberta let me borrow—her mother's brooch." Anna wished she had a mirror to admire her tidy, dark pinstriped suit now embellished with the pearl-encrusted brooch.

After a breakfast of bread and leftovers from yesterday's dinner, the five wandered about the apartment, contemplating what life must be like in the city. In the countryside, it was mostly peaceful, and there were all sorts of places to hide—the barn, the forest, and a trap door. The city was filled with constant noise, from innocent footsteps to gunfire.

Father Kurek signaled the children to follow him as he trudged up the stairs to the attic. "Kitty gave me instructions for us to stay up here in the attic when the group arrives. It's for everyone's safety."

"And Anna?" Elise asked.

"She'll need to be there to receive information about the children. Only Jolanta knows about our mysterious Americans."

"So this Jolanta is really Irena Sendler?" Naomi asked.

Father Kurek nodded with a smile, not understanding that the real Irena Sendler had saved over 3,000 Jewish babies as a social worker during the Holocaust. Naomi made a mental note to tell him the story of this amazing woman after the meeting.

Disappointed not to witness the action downstairs, the children took turns peeking out from the windows onto the street. Instead, they observed the ordinary comings and goings of hundreds of Poles and a few scattered groups of German soldiers.

"So many are carrying babies and large bags that might contain a baby," Elise remarked. Hundreds of people passed, and then a couple with a little girl and some bags appeared to turn into their apartment building. Within a minute, the slight tap on the hallway door signaled their guests had arrived.

Anna opened the door. A petite blonde woman carrying a bundled baby handled all the introductions. "I'm Jolanta. My fellow workers are just behind me." She glanced around the room. "Where can we set the babies?"

Kitty held the door open for another group, which had obviously followed at a distance, and then retrieved the infant from Jolanta's weary arms.

Two young children shuffled in with the adult visitors. "This is Katzryna, two years old, and this one is Artur, age eight. Here are their papers." Jolanta said. "Might it be proper to make a request of Kitty…alone, I mean?"

Kitty escorted Jolanta into the bedroom hallway. "I was given a rather strange story about the unusual children who would help bring these children out of Radom. Is it really true they are invisible?" Jolanta asked.

"The man who is with them calls them angels from the Lord. I know they are in the apartment, but I haven't seen them yet."

"Would it be proper to meet them?" Jolanta asked.

"Come with Anna and me. They're in the attic. You can clearly see the man who came with them. He is masquerading as their uncle."

As they climbed the steps, Kitty alerted the four. "You have a visitor."

Sitting next to the open attic door, Father Kurek had heard the entire conversation. "I'm so glad to meet you. We thought it best not to be in the apartment when you first arrived. Too many people."

"Can these invisible children hear my voice?"

Jolanta asked.

"Oh, yes, and they can also see you," Father Kurek said.

The three children displayed their presence by moving objects around the room.

"Just like the others have said, these children truly are angels. Thank you so much for helping us." Jolanta shook her head to make sense of what she was observing, but not really seeing. "I've recorded the Jewish children's and their parents' names and will keep the list safe. It is my hope their parents might find them after the war."

"Jolanta has saved about two thousand babies from the Warsaw ghetto," Anna said.

Elise's eyes glistened. "I remember reading a book about someone named Irena Sendler who did the same thing." She desperately wanted to let Jolanta know that someday, everyone would one day learn of her heroism. Elise had been cautioned that too much knowledge could lead to mistakes and confusion.

Maria communicated Elise's comments, and Jolanta raised her eyebrows. She was both surprised and confused that Elise knew her real name. "Artur, the eight-year-old, came to me just last night. So far, he's been reticent. The girl is my friend's child and knows me like an aunt. Her mother is a doctor who served with us in the ghetto." Jolanta bit her lip. "It will be hard for me to leave Katzryna. I've known her since birth."

Jolanta continued. "My group must leave now to catch the train back to Warsaw. The babies should sleep several more hours, so you also must leave soon. We'll bring them up here for you to prepare, away from the eyes of the two younger ones. It would be best if the children carried the babies so Artur and Katzryna are unaware of the disguise. The adults should be in charge of the older ones."

"I'm going downstairs to send my friends ahead so I can say goodbye to the children. You can come down as soon as they leave," Jolanta said.

Kitty and Jolanta brought the sleeping babies up to the attic, one by one. Elise and Naomi skillfully wrapped the magical swaddling cloths around the babies. Father Kurek gathered their bags and looked at the children. "Jolanta will have an easier job getting out of the city. Anna and I will take care of the two young children, who might start crying or speaking in Yiddish at any time. Follow closely behind, but only speak if it is an emergency."

He stood at the top of the steps. "By the way, you three did great on the train coming here. Let's ask for God's blessing to make our trip back just as smooth." After hearing the others say goodbye, Father Kurek gave the "coast is clear" signal.

Downstairs, Jolanta tucked a piece of bread in her charge's pockets. "Remember the prayers I taught you, and never say you are Jewish. For now, these two people will be your parents." She pointed to Father Kurek and Anna. "This is Jan and Stacia Grabiec. They will take good care of you."

It was a heartbreaking sight to behold, but everyone understood there was no other option. With tears in her eyes, Irena Sendler and her friends descended the apartment stairs to return to their jobs as social workers in the ghetto.

Chapter Twenty-Two

The Train Trip to Debica

A few dense rays of sun began to sift through the exiting rain clouds when the rescuers started the first leg of their journey to reach the train station. Artur, a slight and skinny child, tightly laced his fingers between Father Kurek's. He was a quiet, pensive child who had obviously been well-trained to protect the truth of his identity. Anna picked up curly-haired Katzryna and told her of the fun they would have on the train ride. Father Kurek nodded, and his entire rescue troop proceeded on their ten-minute walk to the train station in Radom.

Naomi struggled, switching her heavy bundle between each arm as she trudged down the sidewalk. Colin called for Father Kurek to wait so he could put the baby into Naomi's rucksack to carry on his shoulders. It would be one more reason he was grateful for his invisibility. No one would witness the indignity of his wearing a Girl Scout backpack.

Getting to the train station area was more challenging than leaving. Cars waited at the Gestapo barricades for inspection amidst the flurry of activity. Bourgeois-looking families crowded onto the train platform with suitcases while the peasant class lugged their baskets and bundles. A chill ran through Colin's spine as his eyes focused on the most enormous flag he had ever seen, a red one with a black swastika.

With their rifles mounted on their sides, German soldiers patrolled the passengers as they came and went. One leaned against the building post and took a drag from his cigarette. Most seemed more bored than on alert.

The station was a hub for mundane tasks. Passengers reached out the train's window with coins as vendors walked up and down the platform offering hunks of bread for sale. The only thing free was water from pitchers provided by women from the Red Cross. Soldiers surrounded one table at the station and stripped down to their undershirts as they shaved into the water basins.

Amidst some laughing and smiling passengers who appeared not to have a care in the world, were others with expressionless faces. Father Kurek wondered if they, like him, were forced to hide some secret. They could have just as likely been drained of any hope or enthusiasm for life, the kind of emptiness born from too much to bear.

Father Kurek signaled for everyone to sit on the grass far away from the station office while he went inside to purchase the tickets. The children were mildly interested at the sight of passenger and freight trains coming and going. The train's smoke was as thick as moss in the stagnant summer air.

Most unusual was a German troop train with mounted machine guns on the cars carrying tanks and trucks. It slowed as it passed the station with soldiers walking on top of the vehicles.

At the appointed time, the conductor escorted Father Kurek, Anna, Jan, and Katzryna to their first-class compartment on the train but closed the door before

Colin, Elise, and Naomi could board. The three stood on the outside platform in panic.

"Should we push through or wait?" Elise asked.

Anna began to fan herself as she pleaded to the conductor. "Please, leave the door open, please. The air in here is so stifling. Just a few more minutes."

The conductor wrinkled his brows and hesitated. Anna then began to fan herself furiously with a newspaper. "Being pregnant makes a woman's body like a furnace."

"Oh, little Mother, can I bring you some water?" The conductor's previously curt tone swiftly switched to one of compassion.

"Perhaps later. Just the door for now."

Opening the door, he smiled and muttered something about how blessed motherhood was. Colin, Elise, and Naomi scrambled onto the train, collapsing onto the cracked leather seat across from Anna and Father Kurek. Their eyes told one another how fortunate they were to have made it onto the train.

Elise stared at little Katzryna, hugging her doll. She recalled how comforted she felt the day Uncle Józef had given her Ewa, his deceased daughter's doll. She remembered how she sang and cradled that handmade doll in her bright folk outfit. Ewa had been Elise's constant companion during her first time travel adventure. This time, Elise was treated more as an adult with adult-like expectations. She sometimes wished to be pampered again like a child and be allowed to complain about her hunger or exhaustion. Elise winced at the thought of how Americans always carried around water bottles to keep up proper hydration and how any hunger pangs were quickly satisfied. These experiences allowed her to see how most of the world truly lives.

Little Katzryna grew restless and fussed, whining about things that made no sense. She was exhausted, frightened, and missed her parents. Nothing Anna tried calmed the child. Naomi and Elise wished they could have helped distract Katzryna with silly faces or other distractions. Thus far, Katzryna and Artur seemed unaware of the existence of the other children.

The American children noted that rescuing and caring for young Jewish children who were strangers was like handling explosives. Too young to have learned the importance of discretion, they could start crying and calling out in Yiddish. How grateful they were to be given a first-class compartment all to themselves.

With the creaking and humming sounds of the train tracks, Katzryna eventually fell into a deep slumber. Even the periodic stops at various stations didn't jostle her out of sleep. Father Kurek looked at his watch and knew the group's need to switch trains was approaching.

One thing was clear: the babies all needed to be changed. The blankets couldn't hide the foul odor of dirty diapers. Elise's nose crinkled as she fanned her nose. Anna nodded and pointed to the floor. With Katzryna still asleep, the time was now. The three children laid the babies on the ground to unwrap them. Artur's mouth dropped in amazement as he observed invisible hands providing fresh diapers.

"Eww. They didn't teach us how to diaper babies in Girl Scouts." Naomi sputtered. "But I'm getting pretty good at it now."

"What do we do with the dirty cloth diapers?" Elise asked, reflecting on how difficult everything was in the 1940s, especially on a train.

Anna reached out to provide an old, tattered bag. "Jolanta thought of everything."

Artur squinted and rubbed his eyes as he witnessed the mysterious scene. Then, just as suddenly as babies had appeared, they disappeared into thin air. He rubbed his eyes again, shook his head, and uttered in disbelief, "I'm seeing things."

Neither Father Kurek nor Anna reacted to Artur's shock, hoping the boy would believe he had witnessed an illusion.

Father Kurek stood to retrieve his bag, the group's prearranged signal, to continue the necessary deception. "This stop will be where we switch trains." Just as the whistle signaled their arrival, the baby in Elise's arms began to wriggle and let out a few sounds of discomfort.

Anna knew this moment would eventually come. "Elise, unwrap her. I'll carry her from here through the station, and we can feed her."

The groggy Katzryna awakened and resumed her fussing until she saw the baby in Anna's arms. Anna trusted that Katzryna would believe almost anything in this environment. "Katzryna, the baby will enjoy it if you make funny faces when she wakes up fully. You help me, okay?"

Artur now realized something rather supernatural was going on, but not so with Katzryna. The youngster was easily distracted and delighted by the novelty of a baby. In her mind, the baby had just suddenly appeared.

Father Kurek put his arm around Artur. "I'll explain all of this to you when we arrive in Debica, but not now. You'll be amazed when I explain this magic."

Poor Artur lifted his eyebrows and shoulders in resignation and cracked a halfhearted smile. At least

Artur knew he probably wasn't hallucinating.

As the early evening approached, the glare of the sun's intense rays pierced through the train windows as it began its descent into the western skies. The train screeched to a halt as passengers lined the platform for the nighttime trip, waiting impatiently. Fortunately, far more people exited the train, promising a less stressful ride. Of course, the night was not immune to the same avalanche of misfortune as they had witnessed the night before.

Thus far, the trip had been exhausting, with only a few chunks of bread and a small bag of boiled potatoes to satisfy the hungry group. As soon as they deboarded the train, Father Kurek began searching for the assigned platform for the final leg of their journey.

Elise and Naomi gave each other's arms a much-needed rest by taking turns carrying their charges. Anna marveled at their spirit of steadfastness and devotion to their task. The children could have so easily withered in spirit and purposely let the cell phone battery wear down. Returning to the safety and ease of life in America would have been an understandable choice for anyone. Instead, they chose to share Poland's burden.

Their train was scheduled to depart in a half-hour, so Father Kurek had just enough time to purchase a few food supplies to tide them over to Debica and fill their canteens. He decided that everyone's energy needed to be sustained, so he bought dried fruits, croissants, and cheese for their journey. He filled the milk bottles at a corner table and then sprinted back to his charges.

Anna and the children walked back and forth on the wooden platform to stretch their legs, enjoying the small freedom of moving about before boarding. Talking directly to the Americans was nearly impossible, so speaking in a vague code was all Anna could do. "I don't quite know what to do about baby Inka here. Perhaps I'll wrap her back up in the special blanket once we board the train. It's best to wait until she has her privacy, right?"

Father Kurek greeted the railway official with a tired smile and a polite "good evening" as he turned over their travel documents and the children's birth records. The conductor luridly inspected Anna from head to toe. "So young to have three children who look so different."

Anna's legs suddenly felt weak as she clutched the baby closer. "Sir, these two children are my niece and nephew. We are escorting them to stay with their grandparents in Mielec. Only the baby is ours."

"Have these two show me they are good Catholics. Now," the surly official said as he kept his eyes on Anna.

Anna breathed in deeply, feeling the rise and fall of her chest, telling herself to remain calm. The children had recited their prayers on the train with her just an hour ago. But that was while they felt safe, not under this type of malicious interrogation.

"These are good Polish children who know their prayers," Anna pleaded.

The children had been well trained and automatically slapped their hands together in prayer and began to recite, "Our Father, who art in Heaven, hallowed…"

"Stop! Stop." With a dismissive wave of his hand, the man was satisfied. "Get on your train."

"Thank you. Thank you…" Father Kurek gratefully nodded his head to the ticket-taker and then, once out of earshot, muttered, "Damn Teuton."

A kindlier conductor escorted Anna and the children up the train car's steps, where they were startled to see a German SS officer in their compartment. The man glanced up and rattled his newspaper. Clearly perturbed, he furrowed his eyebrows and snarled. He continued to mutter about how the silence surely would be shattered by the presence of children, Polish ones at that.

The conductor's face flushed, and he was rattled. "Sir, can I offer you a cup of coffee? Or a cool glass of water?"

The group hesitated to enter, hoping the conductor had made a mistake, but he gently shrugged his shoulders. "Plenty of room in this car, ma'am. I'm sorry that we cannot provide the private compartment as promised. But, look. The little one can even stretch out to sleep."

The group shuffled into the car, resigned to a threatening reality. They would be under the scrutiny of the worst of Germany, an SS officer trained to detect deception and Jews. Katzryna shuffled into the compartment and backed as far away from the officer as possible, clinging to Anna's skirt. The Americans with the babies sat on the floor, far away from the officer.

Katzryna frantically crawled all over Father Kurek, like she was scaling a mountain, trying to be as far away from the German as possible. The young child clearly understood that people dressed in those uniforms only brought bad things. Terror had been an unfortunate side of her young life inside the ghetto.

"Forgive us. The child is tired and hasn't slept." Father Kurek explained as Katzryna continued to thrash about inconsolably. As typically happens, the crying became contagious. The infant in Anna's arms began to howl in sharp, earsplitting wails. Baby Leib was named accurately. His scream seemed quite a bit like a lion's roar.

The Nazi growled and threw his newspaper to the floor and stood to gather his bag. "I'd rather sit in third class with the peasants." Colin, Elise, and Naomi quickly smashed themselves into a corner so the angry German could exit. They still didn't know whether the outside world could be bumped into and were not eager to find out. The officer stormed out of the compartment and shouted for the conductor to find him a more peaceful location.

The children collapsed into the upholstered seat with their still-sleeping charges. Each subsequent stop put everyone on alert as they wondered if another threatening person might burst into the compartment. Eventually, the other two babies awakened and were fed, changed, and returned to the American children. Katzryna and Artur slept a few hours on the empty benches. Anna and Father Kurek managed only a few interludes of slumber. The babies lay on top of their bags so the children's arms could rest. Poor Artur muttered in his sleep, uttering desperate phrases in Yiddish. Father Kurek could only imagine what would have happened to them all if the Nazi officer had remained in their midst.

Chapter Twenty-Three

A House in the Wilderness

The first threads of daylight wove their way through the window as the train pulled into the next station. Father Kurek stretched and sighed heavily, giving thanks to God for a safe journey thus far. "Anna, the next stop will be ours. It's time to get everyone prepared."

The children all let out a collective moan and went about taking care of their needs. Colin scrunched his nose. "My mouth is foul. I wish I could brush my teeth."

Elise's face flew into Colin's. "We all smell. But don't worry. There aren't any pretty girls here that you need to impress."

Naomi was indignant. "Hey, what about me?"

Colin sneered. "I'm your cousin. I don't need to look or smell nice for a cousin."

"Well, if pretty young girls were around, none of them could see you anyway. Although I also wonder if pretty girls of Colin's age could smell stinky breath right now?" Anna smirked, and the two girls giggled. She was pleased that almost everyone could still find something to smile about.

"Here's our final stop. Everyone ready?" Father Kurek asked as he guided his group off the train.

They stepped off onto a rugged wooden platform guarded by only one uninterested soldier sitting on a stool. Unlike the other stations, this one had no town but instead led into a wilderness with only shabby wooden homes dotting the forked road.

Father Kurek pointed to a road bordered by birch trees. "It should be on the road to the left. We walk past ten houses and then go into the vacant house with the broken gate. House number 56."

Colin ran up to join Father Kurek and Artur. "Do you know who will be there to meet us?"

The priest turned his head to Colin and whispered. "Wait until we're alone." Colin began to think like a member of a cell once again in the Home Army. He suspected the rescue would likely involve some partisans from the forests. While Artur seemed likable, no one outside a partisan cell could be trusted with information that might put another's life at risk. If their group was arrested, the Germans weren't above torturing children, especially Jews, to secure partisans' location and identities.

Father Kurek noted the contrast between Colin, who was so willing to help, and Artur, who never bothered to ask if he could help. "Artur, you're a strong boy. Why don't you carry little Katzryna for a while? The house shouldn't be too far."

The toddler was happy to have anyone carry her, and his help left Father Kurek free to speak to Colin. "I only know what I've been told: wait at that vacant house. My cell contact told me a candle would be inside the tea kettle in the cupboard. That will tell us we are in the correct place and the situation is safe."

The group trudged up the road with all three babies now awake and whimpering.

Naomi slogged down the path. "How far is this

house? My arm is going to break right off."

"I'm sorry, Naomi. You must be so tired. I can carry her now." Father Kurek slung his pack over his left shoulder and cradled the baby in his other arm. Elise ran up to walk next to the priest. "I've noticed that Katzryna doesn't seem to notice that you are talking to us and hasn't asked who you and Anna are talking to."

"I've noticed that too, but maybe it is because she is so confused, and nothing seems real to her," Father Kurek replied.

"Maybe it is because she is like a little kid who thinks make-believe is real and doesn't know the difference."

Father Kurek laughed. "Or maybe Elise, Katzryna thinks something is really wrong with us and is too kind to mention that we are strange people who talk to ourselves."

"Now, that's funny," Elise chuckled and then pointed to a house with broken windows that was obviously vacant. "That's the ninth house, but I don't see any number signs on any of them."

"The numbers are mostly for the county's land records," Anna said. "Who would put a number on a house? All your neighbors know who lives there."

"How does the mailman keep the houses straight when he makes a delivery?" Colin asked.

"A mailman? We've no mailman coming to our homes. We go to the post office in town for our mail. Sometimes, a trusted neighbor picks up any mail." Anna shrugged her shoulders. "We get almost no mail anymore."

"So, in America, you have a mailman who brings mail to your house every week?" Father Kurek smiled and imagined how privileged it must be for a postman to bring mail to each home. "Our relatives in America know it isn't safe for us to receive much mail from them. Besides, anything of value would be stolen."

"No, Father Kurek, we get mail delivered to our house every day. Except Sunday. Oh, holidays, too. No mail then," Elise responded.

"What a wonderful place America must be to live! Mail delivered every day." Father Kurek shook his head in amazement.

The group had just passed house number ten and stood in front of the eleventh. In its orchard were apple and plum trees with their twisted branches already bearing fruit.

"Can we take some fruit?" Elise asked.

"Let's first see if this is the right place." Father Kurek signaled for everyone to stay at the broken gate. The house's untended pastures sat silently with no signs of livestock, and the garden's weeds had already won the war amongst the patches of raspberries. The place certainly seemed vacant.

Father Kurek padded up the grassy path to the door and then knocked, but there was no response. "Let me check out back before we go in." The priest returned to the front and signaled that the house was indeed abandoned. Anna turned to survey the other homes for signs of farmers. She then noted a woman from the house across the road peering from her window. The curtain quickly fell into place, and the woman disappeared. So typical of villagers who know everything that is going on in the nearby homes. Anna thought about her mother, who had a sixth sense for detecting news and gossip. It was her father, though, who spread it to his confidants at the tavern. Anna feared this woman might be one of those who turned in any news of strangers to the Germans. Another reason to pray.

The children scampered into the home, happy to be safe for at least a little while. It was curious that the inside was left in a rather tidy manner. Most of the furniture and household items one might expect to see in an occupied house sat waiting for their owners' return.

"My house!" Katzryna brightened as she ran through the home, assuming her long journey had come to an end.

Father Kurek opened the cupboard, and there was a kettle. A water kettle such as this was always kept on the stove, so he was confident it contained the candle. He let out a sigh and held the small candle up. "This is the right house. Thank you, Jesus."

Artur shuffled to the table and lay his head down to rest. Father Kurek pointed to a more private sleeping area at the back of the home. "Why don't you see if that big chest has some bedding? Go rest on that bed. You too, Katzryna." The little one skipped to the bed with her doll underneath one arm. Artur groaned at the need to share his bed with the energetic child.

"What are we going to do with these babies? They'll be hungry in a few hours." Elise said.

"A woman across the street was staring at us through the window and must have seen Katzryna. It can't hurt to ask her for milk. It's just as risky as having howling babies here." Anna replied.

Colin remembered how he had learned to milk a cow at the Bryks' house in Niwiska. "How about if I go milk a neighbor's cow?" Colin suggested. "No one will know, except the cow."

"We'll only do that if we're desperate. You might spook the cow, and then who knows what would happen?" Father Kurek suggested.

Elise brushed the dusty curtain to the side so she could get a better look at a man bridling his horse onto his cart. "Father Kurek, there's a man across the road. It looks like he might be getting ready to take a trip in his cart."

Anna and Father Kurek ran to the window just in time to see the cart turn onto the road.

"He has nothing in his cart."

Anna's heart began to race.

Father Kurek gritted his teeth. "Maybe he's going to report us to the Germans. We'd be worth at least a dozen eggs and a link of sausage to him."

"What story should we give the Germans if they arrive?" Anna asked. She and the priest had yet to settle on a plausible reason for their presence if soldiers came pounding on the door. What would sound believable? That they had decided to bring two children and three babies to live in the wilderness? Only Jews would be desperate enough to do such a thing. By now, most of the local Polish farmers forced to evacuate had likely found housing elsewhere.

Father Kurek sat in his usual pensive way, his finger resting thoughtfully against his lips. Anna found the silence a bit unsettling; she preferred to voice her thoughts openly, inviting discussion rather than keeping them bottled up.

"How about this," Father Kurek finally said. "We say we were living with my brother, but his youngest developed what we suspect is typhus. To protect everyone, we left the house and brought his two babies along with ours."

Anna added, "And we had heard about this house sitting vacant, so we came to see if it was truly empty."

Father Kurek began to rethink their strategy. "We don't have to say anything about the babies. Just keep the door open for Colin, Elise, and Naomi to take the babies outside."

"Yes. Yes. Only two children make more sense. Artur can be a child from my first marriage, and Katzryna can be ours."

"You two should just get married," Naomi offered. "Since you are a priest, you can marry yourself, right?"

Anna's beet-red face was the only signal Naomi needed to know she should be silent.

Elise's eyes rolled as she quickly pulled her cousin aside. "Naomi, priests don't get married. *Ever*."

Naomi, ever the romantic eleven-year-old, was undeterred. "Well, they make a nice couple, anyway."

For the next two hours, everyone rehearsed the story they would give if the Nazis did show up. For now, it was just lovely to enjoy a few minutes of peace inside the house.

Chapter Twenty-Four
Partisans

The children gathered more wood from the pile stacked beside the cottage so Anna could cook soup with the potatoes and carrots she'd discovered in the cupboard. The carrots were firm, as if freshly pulled from the earth, and beside them sat a jar of lard. The rich, savory pork fat would make the soup thicker and more filling, a small luxury in these times.

What unsettled Anna was how the cottage looked lived-in, almost cared for. The shelves weren't bare, the floor was swept, yet the gardens and meadow outside had been abandoned for at least a month. It was too intact... as if whoever had left might return at any moment.

She couldn't help thinking of last spring, when the Germans had driven her family from their home in Niwiska. The place her father found in the wilderness back then had been a shell, looted, filthy, and stripped of anything useful. Her mother Maria's heart had given out under the strain, leaving her bedridden for weeks. That memory sat heavy in Anna's chest as she stirred the pot.

Colin, stationed as lookout, spoke in a low voice. "Father Kurek, now the woman's going to the barn."

The priest joined him at the narrow gap in the curtain.

"There she is," Colin continued. "Now she's carrying a bottle... and something in paper."

Anna's stomach knotted. These days, every stranger's movement was a question mark. Would it mean help or harm?

"She's walking this way," Colin whispered.

Father Kurek snapped the curtain closed and stepped aside, signaling for silence. The air in the room thickened; even the children's shuffling stopped.

Then came the sound, three slow knocks. Heavy. Measured.

The floorboards seemed to groan in reply, and somewhere in the corner a spoon clinked softly against a pot as Anna froze. Outside, a faint creak of boots on the porch.

Then…nothing.

"She's gone," Colin murmured. He slowly opened the door and saw items she had left for them. "She obviously doesn't want to interact with us."

Father Kurek unwrapped the paper: a chunk of sausage. Colin held up the bottle of milk.

"She must have seen the children and taken pity on us," Anna said, relief edging into her voice.

Colin shook his head. "Maybe. But it doesn't mean her husband would feel the same. She could be kind-hearted and still know exactly what he plans to do."

"You think like a Pole, Colin," Father Kurek said quietly. A grim note settled in his voice. In wartime, even the young learned quickly. Kindness might be genuine, or it might be bait. Until tested, no stranger could be trusted.

"We'll feed the babies and then eat while we all have a chance. The others sit and enjoy a chunk of this sausage while I pour the soup," Anna said.

Artur wrinkled his nose at the piece of meat on the

clay plate. "No, I don't want any."

"If he doesn't want it, then I'll take it!" Naomi volunteered. "But why don't you like sausage?"

"Artur, I know most Jews don't eat pork meat," Father Kurek offered. "You must learn to eat pork if you're to pass as a Catholic. Don't make your situation more difficult than it already is."

"I can't. It makes me nauseous," Artur said.

Maria had sympathy for Artur, who had grown up with the feeling of intense repulsion for any pork product.

The clopping of the horse and cart's rattle echoed from a distance. Father Kurek alerted the others. "The man has returned, and two others are with him. Cover up the babies and take them outside."

Colin, Elise, and Naomi covered their charges and rushed out the back door. Two men jumped out of the cart before the farmer slowly turned into his property.

Father Kurek braced himself as he considered the possibilities. Could they be Volksdeutsch hired to investigate for the Gestapo? "They aren't soldiers." Father Kurek cracked open the door. "All of you stay at the table, and I'll go outside to talk with them."

The priest slowly opened the door. "Father Kurek!" one of the men shouted. The priest's heart jumped when he recognized Józef Bryk, his closest friend from Niwiska. His thin, somewhat gangly frame was easily discernible. They embraced, and the priest hurried the two men inside. He whispered, "Anna, tell the children it's safe to come in. Their Uncle Józef is here!"

Before anyone started to talk freely, Father Kurek covertly signaled everyone not to share identities or plans. "Artur, take Katzryna out to the back of the house for some fresh air." Confused, the two obediently exited the back door.

Anna closed the door behind Artur and Katzryna and turned to her cousin Józef. "We were so worried when the farmer left in his cart. We thought he was ratting us out to the Germans."

Colin and Elise's eyes brightened upon seeing Józef again. Elise raced to embrace him. "Uncle Józef!"

"My precious Elise, and there's my sweet Naomi again!" They both melted into his arms with a look of contentment on their faces. "Florian and I came to escort you to your next stops."

Florian stepped forward to kiss Naomi's hand. "I'm the nephew of your Cudecki grandparents, so we are also related." Naomi giggled at the gallant Florian. His good looks and dark curly hair would knock anyone off their feet, especially an impressionable young girl.

When Florian kissed her hand, Elise returned his gesture with a smile. She had grown accustomed to the good manners of Polish men.

Józef smiled broadly. "In case you didn't pick up on this, Simon and Veronica across the road are amongst the many in this area who help the AK. This house is where we come for supplies and sometimes sleep. The villagers here are the eyes, ears, and hands of the Home Army."

"Why didn't they just tell us what was going on?" Elise asked.

"These people faithfully provide. Their identity must be protected just like the AK partisans in the forest."

"So, there are no traitors like Mishka around here?" Colin asked. "He's the one we're really worried about since he can see us."

"Anyone can turn dark, but as far as we know, these villagers have been very loyal to the AK." Józef poured himself a cup of grain coffee.

Florian scoffed. "No one needs to worry about Mishka anymore. He had an accident."

The adults understood what was meant by the inflection in Józef's voice. Anna put her hand to her mouth.

"What kind of accident?" Elise asked.

"All you need to know is that he was taken care of." Those who hadn't seen the atrocities of war could never understand. The adults recognized the need to take a stand against those who threatened the lives of innocent people with their treachery and betrayal. You either fought against the Germans and those who aligned themselves with the Reich, or you were the enemy. Kill or be killed.

Józef could see the conflicted looks on the children's faces. How could Americans fully understand the evil forces that enveloped their lives? How could a Polish citizen gladly provide information on the actions of the Home Army to the Germans? How could Mishka endanger Sister Aniela, his own flesh and blood, for a bottle of German liquor or a dozen eggs to sell on the black market? "Elise, that's what happens to those who betray their country. We know people who were executed after Mishka reported them to the Germans as Home Army collaborators. He is responsible for many deaths of innocent people."

Ever the charming gentleman, Florian knew it was time to change the somber mood. He pulled out a loaf of bread from his rucksack. "My mother made this for Anna and the children."

Seeing a loaf of beautifully shaped rye bread, Colin, Elise, and Naomi's eyes lit up. They had learned to appreciate the savory smell and taste of such a bread that could sustain them the entire day.

"I'll be taking Father Kurek and the Jewish children to their next stop. We need to leave very soon," Florian said.

Józef added, "The trip with the babies will take longer. We're taking backroads and will leave early tomorrow morning. Simon will let us use his cart, and he'll supply us with milk for the babies. Veronica is preparing your dinner as we speak."

"Do we get to meet that beautiful princess tomorrow?" Naomi asked.

Józef chuckled. "I hope you're not disappointed, Naomi. Helena Jabłonowska is as old as Sister Roberta, but I must admit, she does seem quite regal."

Father Kurek smiled, remembering all the reports about Helena's work for the local people. "Helena is beautiful on both the inside and outside. She could have run off to a safe country before the war, but chose to stay here. Florian, do you know that Helena's the reason we were able to ride in first-class accommodations on the train?"

Anna lifted the basket of soiled diapers and wriggled her nose. "Enough talk. We need to wash out the babies' cloth diapers before our journey. Who'd like to join me at the well in the back of the house?"

Chapter Twenty-Five

Off to Meet Helena Jabłonowska

It was the kind of morning a person might forget to worry if it hadn't been for the war. Small white birds swooped up to the fluffy white clouds. The crowd of roosters echoed from faraway farms as the early sunlight arrowed through the trees.

The forest path dotted with spruce and pines might have been enough for Józef to overlook his wartime burdens. With seven others to protect, his mind needed to stay laser-focused as he guided the horse and cart through the back roads. Walking on foot through the woods would have been far safer if he had been making the journey alone. He could have escaped far into the forest if there was the slightest concern.

The group decided it was best to have nothing in the cart with the children. If stopped by the Germans, they could simply jump off the back of the cart and walk farther down the road or run in the woods until it was safe to rejoin Józef and Anna. Although invisible, any movement of the hay would trigger suspicion.

Poland had become increasingly bleak for Colin and Elise. Their previous adventure somehow seemed safer. Living at the family house in Niwiska, they lived in a relatively safe dwelling surrounded by a loving family. Rescuing Jewish children gave them an insight into the dark world of the Holocaust, where all Jews and those who made any attempt to save them were hunted. Elise remembered how, before she ever traveled to Poland, her grandmother told her she thought the country would be in shades of black and white, all drab gray with no color. After her first visit, she changed her mind. Elise agreed with her grandmother that Poland's countryside was the most beautiful place on earth.

Józef was aware of the various groups they might encounter at any time. Some of the most brutal soldiers from neighboring Ukraine and Estonia came to Camp Heidelager for their SS training. Bands of thieves and social outcasts roamed the forests, looking to take advantage of anyone unfortunate enough to be in their path. And then there were a few locals like Mishka who might instigate all sorts of havoc. The only friendly people were the Home Army partisans who filled the forests surrounding Camp Heidelager.

As Józef scanned the countryside, he sometimes wondered about what seemed like silhouettes of soldiers in faraway trees. It was usually only shadows. He saw a mirage of dust, and soon, a truck's motor's expected roar spelled impending doom for the travelers. Józef's heart sank. They were so close, just north of Debica. The Germans would likely pull them over for inspection.

All the possibilities raced through Józef's mind. Would the Germans be ones he knew from the forestry service? Might he and Anna pass as just a married couple traveling to care for a sick parent? Or would they be taken to Gestapo headquarters in Debica for questioning?

The children scooched close to the back of the cart so they could jump off before the babies began to whimper. As Józef pulled back on the reins to slow down, he went through his mental checklist of what to do if stopped by a German. Relax your shoulders and the muscles in your face. Say as little as possible. Don't volunteer any information. Present the situation in terms that might be deemed an acceptable reason to be out on the roads.

Anna pulled out her handkerchief in case it might be appropriate to dab her teary eyes. Of course, the officer would not have any compassion, but her action might assist whatever story Józef gave. First, they'd have to read the situation.

The German truck slowed as it approached, and the driver issued a hand signal for Józef and Anna to stop for inspection. The young soldier in the passenger seat sprang out of the truck. Filled with bravado and brashness, he strutted to the cart and ordered both Józef and Anna off the cart." The driver, a slightly older man, stood back and counted on his subordinate's towering bulk to intimidate the Poles. He leaned against the running truck to observe the interaction.

The three children slithered down the back of the cart and slowly walked with the babes in their arms to the grassy areas leading to the forests. They huddled beneath the grove of beech trees lining the road at a safe distance. Elise trembled and laid the baby down on the bough of green. The three hovered together as they watched the Germans inspect Józef and Anna's papers. Horrified, the children observed the Germans shoving Józef and Anna toward the truck. The soldiers forced the couple into the back of the vehicle.

The truck roared past the children, leaving a cloud of dust as it gradually disappeared. The birds fluttered from tree to tree. The forest area was then totally silent, as were the children. Their minds whirled with worries about Józef and Anna.

"What will we do if the Germans take Józef and Anna to town?" Elise whispered. "Right now, I'm more worried about them hurting Józef and Anna." Naomi whimpered. The children just looked at one another, seemingly helpless and utterly alone.

"Now what?" Colin asked. "Do we take the cart, or do we walk?"

"If we take the cart, and someone sees it, they'll be very suspicious," Elise said.

"The horse is still attached to it, so maybe the person will think it just took off running with no driver." Colin shrugged. "Let's wait just a bit and see if Anna and Józef return."

"We can wait just a few minutes." Elise blew out a deep breath. "We're partisans, and a partisan considers their mission first. Ours is to bring these babies to Countess Jablonowska. Either we walk, or Józef and Anna have to walk. These babies aren't going to stay calm forever, and they'll need to be fed soon."

"We don't know where this manor house is located. We can't drive around the back roads until we see a sign saying "Jablonowski Manor House," Naomi said.

"You're getting pretty smart about wartime problems, Naomi," Elise said.

Colin held up Naomi's phone. "I've already thought of that. I found the Jablonowski house on maps."

"So, we just go there by ourselves? Three invisible people just coming up to the Countess?" Naomi frowned. "How's that going to work since we can't talk to her?"

"I suppose she's expecting us." Elise shrugged her

shoulders. "And it's not like we have any other options."

"Let's get going. You two will have to take care of the babies while I drive the cart." Colin said.

"Wait a minute. I'm the one who knows how to ride a horse, so I'd be better at controlling the reins." Elise said.

"Really?" Colin cocked his head and condescendingly raised his eyebrows. He then remembered Wojciech's temperamental personality and how Elise's gentle but commanding touch seemed to calm him. "Okay, I'll let you try to control him. Just don't run us into a tree."

Elise wished she had more confidence, but her experience with horses was only as a rider. "First, you have to let a horse know who's boss." She untangled the reins from the tree and guided Wojciech to the road, calmly stroking his body the whole time. "It's okay, Wojciech. I know those Germans were scary, but everything is okay. We're going to get out of here and get you some water and food."

Elise held the horse steady while Colin and Naomi climbed onto the cart. "Now, if only someone would hold me steady." She climbed onto the seat and picked up the reins. "Let's go, Wojciech," was all the horse needed to trot down the dusty road.

"This map app is amazing. I just hope the roads now and this map from the future match up." Colin said. "Elise, in just a bit, you'll see a fork in the road. Go to the right."

Elise kept trying to remind herself that Wojciech could probably sense the tension in her hands on his reins. "Got that, Wojciech? I sure hope steering a cart is the same as when you're on top of a horse."

"I wonder what's happening to Anna and Józef?" Naomi asked Colin.

Colin put one of the babies over his shoulder. "Let's not think about it. Keep your focus on the babies. We have enough to worry about."

Chapter Twenty-Six

The Manor House

"That must be the Jablonowski house." Colin held the cell phone up to show Elise as she pulled back on the reins. They surveyed the white home's expansive front with charming gables and hip roof, looking more suited to a remote mountain resort than the wilderness. The willows, evergreens, and shrubbery bordering the expansive lawn stretched down the slight hill and seemed to embrace the house.

"Check out this photo of what the house looks like in the future." Colin showed Elise and Naomi the pictures on the cell phone of the once-proud manor home. It would someday lie in ruins with years of neglect eating away at it. "The Germans and Russians took turns destroying the house when the war was almost over. The story said the Russians took the land and house away from the Jablonowskis."

Elise guided Wojciech on the narrow road leading to the stables. The Countess had obviously anticipated their arrival. She hurried to the back courtyard to greet her guests, but stopped in her tracks when she recognized the cart had no passengers.

Her butler, Antoni, inspected the cart. "No, nothing, Pani Jablonowska. How in the world would a horse know its way to our stables?"

"Where are Józef and Anna, and the three children?"

"What do we do, guys? They need some sort of signal from us." Elise lifted the reins high in the air. Naomi and Colin jumped from the cart, stirring up a small dust cloud to show their location. Then, Naomi mischievously tapped the butler, who almost jumped a foot off the ground.

"Antoni, should we assume what we see is evidence of the invisible American children?" the Countess whispered. "But where are Józef and Anna?"

Elise unwrapped one of the babies and brought her to Helena. The sleepy babe wriggled her nose and commenced to erupt into a shrill cry, waking the other two. Naomi reached into her Girl Scout pack and retrieved the empty bottles to give to the butler.

"This is just all so bizarre. How will we ever communicate if Józef or Anna aren't here?" Countess Jablonowska stroked the base of her neck as her mind searched for answers. "Oh, dear. There is so much I don't know about these invisible American children. But, I heard that the children ate real food." She clasped her hands together and looked side to side. "I hope you can hear me, children. Please come in and sit so we can offer proper hospitality."

As the Countess climbed up the stairs, two maids rushed out to the portico to see the babies. "Oh, this is one of the little ones we have been expecting. Antoni, bring those bottles to the kitchen so we can wash them properly. Don't you worry, little ones. We have a fresh pitcher of milk waiting for you in the kitchen."

The servants' entrance was the children's introduction to the magnificent Polish manor house. The family's esteemed heritage was on full display, with portraits of ancestors proudly displayed alongside paintings of Poland's historical battles and uprisings. In the elegant dining room, adorned with swords above the fireplace, were porcelain vases and statues in every nook and cranny.

The study was the room of perhaps the most remarkable contrast to the average villager's humble home. Many villagers were illiterate and owned only a few books if a younger family member could read. In the Jablonowski's study were hundreds of books bound in leather that graced the fine oak shelves. A large standing globe in the middle of the room gave testimony to the educated classes' opportunities and social position. Two comfortable leather chairs sat on each side of the fireplace, waiting for some member of the family to settle in for a long evening of reading.

Colin strode to the massive carved desk and pulled out the chair. He began to write an explanation of what happened to Józef and Anna. Helena entered and saw the ink pen dip into the ink bottle on its own. She then stood next to the occupied chair to read the letter.

"So, you think it was the Gestapo who took Józef and Anna?" the Countess asked.

Colin wrote, "I think they were just soldiers, but I can't for sure tell the difference between the Gestapo and a regular German soldier. Sorry."

"You did the right thing by bringing the children here quickly. My staff will take them to their temporary homes right after they are fed and changed." Colin pushed the letter closer to her, and she managed to touch his hand. "How amazing that I can feel your hand and your arm even though I can't see them." She patted his hand, "Thank you so much for your bravery. We don't normally expect our children to get involved in these activities. My sons are all serving in the underground army, but they are a bit older than you. We are inspired by your bravery. Of all the good character traits God has given us, courage is the most important. Unfortunately. It is also the rarest."

The countess then took the paper and threw it into the fireplace's flames. "Never leave traces of our cell's work, right?"

How Colin wished he could have a long conversation. He wanted to ask the Countess about her activities and how her life had changed since the war. Of course, burning their written conversation reminded him it was always unwise to put anything down on paper.

From the window next to the desk, Colin saw two people whizzing down the road on bicycles. "There's Józef and Anna!" He and the Countess rushed to the courtyard to see them dismount their bikes and rush to the children.

"Józef! Anna! Are we relieved to see you!" Elise said.

"Fortunately, when we arrived at the Gestapo headquarters, Colonel Heiss from Niwiska was there. He vouched for us." Józef wiped the perspiration from his forehead with his neck scarf. "Having a mother and sister who are forced to work as his cooks certainly paid off. He loves my mother's cooking."

"Sorry that we left you without a ride back," Colin said. "Did they drive you back to the cart?"

Anna smiled and then drank some of the cool spring water offered. "The Gestapo doesn't extend that sort of courtesy to Poles. We were just allowed to leave."

"We were never alone, though, and you three

weren't either. The partisans in the forest quickly found us. They had also been trailing you from the time the Germans took us until the moment you reached here. They were very impressed that the cart with ghosts made it safely to the manor house." Józef guffawed as he imagined the sight of an unoccupied cart trotting down the path without a person at the reins. "And they were very impressed with the driver."

"You mean we were safe all the time?" Naomi asked.

"Of course, reconnaissance is part of a partisan's job. They had guns to protect you, too."

Naomi beamed. "Wow, we must be really important to have armed bodyguards!"

Chapter Twenty-Seven

Naomi

Elise and Colin wandered to find their cousin so she could join them. The countess was serving delicious-looking food in the dining room. Naomi slumped down on the sofa in the library and then curled up in a ball. Naomi certainly wasn't her usual bouncy self. She usually enjoyed walking around any new place and checking out the decorations. Countess Jablonowska's home was like a museum.

"Naomi, there are so many dishes I think you would love. Those noodles and sausage are delicious, and you would love the cold beets."

"No thanks. My stomach doesn't feel so good." Naomi said. "I just want to sleep." Naomi buried her head in the corner of the sofa. How she wished she could just lie in a comfortable bed and surrender to a deep sleep.

"I don't think the Countess would like your feet on her sofa," Elise said.

"Elise," Colin said with a condescending drone. "Nobody here can even see us, so it doesn't matter. Maybe Naomi has a cold or something."

"What's wrong with Naomi?" Anna asked as she entered the library.

"She's probably just exhausted. This trip has to be

hard on a little kid like her," Colin answered.

Naomi didn't react to Colin's comment. She typically would have snarled and told him she wasn't a little kid.

"Sweetheart. What's wrong?" Anna sat next to Naomi on the sofa and brushed the wisps of hair out of her eyes. Naomi's forehead was beading with sweat. "Naomi is burning up."

Naomi just moaned, seeming too exhausted to care.

"Colin, go find Józef and the Countess. Elise, ask the cook for a wet napkin and bring it to me."

Józef sprinted into the room when he overheard the news about Naomi. Anna placed the wet napkin on Naomi's forehead. "Józef, Naomi has a fever and isn't at all herself."

Józef grew frantic. "What are the possibilities? Any other symptoms?"

"I don't know. I wonder if there's a doctor in the village?" Anna asked.

Józef bolted up the stairs to the bedroom area to find the Countess. "Helena, little Naomi has a fever and appears to be quite ill." After explaining the symptoms, the Countess instructed the butler to go to Debica, hoping to find the doctor.

Józef's worries reached back to this past winter when his sister Maria and his adopted young daughter both fell ill from typhus. Fever and exhaustion descended upon both of them like a bolt of lightning. Maria recovered, but little Janina passed away after just a few days. He couldn't bear to think this brave little partisan might have picked up typhus from one of the babies or from the primitive living conditions to which she was exposed for the last weeks.

Countess Jablonowska insisted Naomi be placed in the coolest bedroom with a northerly breeze.

"Do you want me to read to you, Naomi?" Elise asked.

Naomi lifted her head slightly and then lay back down in exhaustion. "I don't care."

A Jewish physician, Dr. Anderson, arrived and entered the room with Countess Jablonowska and Anna within an hour. His thin, dark hair and gray tweed suit gave him a rather refined presence. "I still can't quite believe I'm treating an invisible child, but if the Countess insists the patient is real, how could I refuse?"

Elise lowered the bed covering to show the doctor that someone was really in the bed. Dr. Anderson gave Anna a glass thermometer. "Slip this under her tongue for a few minutes." The doctor witnessed the thermometer bob up and down every few seconds as Naomi attempted to keep it in her mouth.

'One hundred and three." The doctor raised his eyebrows. "Now, describe what the symptoms are. Do you see any red spots or other discolorations on the skin?

Anna brushed the locks of sweaty hair from Naomi's forehead. "Sweetheart, sit up so I can check your back and tummy. No one except Elise and I can see you."

"There's something like a red rash and a few bumps on the stomach and chest, and also a few bumps on her back. She's been very unlike herself for the last few hours. Some nausea but no vomiting."

"This is so difficult. It could be influenza or something, maybe more serious."

"Let's talk outside," Anna said. "Elise, you stay with your cousin."

Doctor Anderson rifled through his medical bag and pulled out two different medications. One was to bring down the fever, and the other was to reduce acid, as he believed flu germs could only survive in an acid environment. "These are the only things I have that might work. She really needs an antibiotic, but those are as rare as hen's teeth."

"What exactly does she have?" Anna asked.

"It could be anything from influenza to strep throat or even typhus. Just keep the child cool and offer tea. If her stomach can handle it, perhaps some garlic." The doctor could see the exasperation on the women's faces. "I'm sorry. There is so little available to us, and certainly, we can't take an invisible child to a hospital."

Elise stood near the door to overhear the adults with Naomi's cell phone in her hand. She waited for Anna to return to Naomi before she rushed to find Colin.

Colin was sitting in the courtyard petting the Jablonowski's retriever. The dog didn't seem bothered that he couldn't see who was petting him and even leaned in to rest his head on Colin's lap.

"Colin, we need to find out what's wrong with Naomi. The doctor mentioned it could be influenza, strep throat, or typhus, and typhus is what killed Józef's little girl last winter!" Elise powered up the phone. We have thirty percent left on Naomi's phone."

The siblings first checked out an article on strep throat. Colin read off a list of symptoms and then the treatments. "That looks really bad, and even if she survives without antibiotics, she might be left with severe heart problems."

Elise began to tear up. "We know she could die from typhus. That is what all the Jews are worried about in the ghettos."

Colin and Elise looked at each other, with the cell phone power down to 20 percent. Elise pursed her lips, trying to restrain her tears. "It's time to say goodbye to everyone. We really need to power down soon."

"We don't have a choice, Elise. Don't feel bad." Colin put his arm around his little sister.

"I'm not sad about leaving. What if we arrive home too late?" Elise wiped her damp eyes with her sleeve. "Let's go find Anna and Józef."

Anna was leaving the kitchen with a freshened cooling towel. "Anna, where is Józef? We need to talk to both of you together," Elise said.

"Józef is sitting with Naomi," Anna said.

"I think Naomi can hear what we have to say," Elise said as they walked to the bedroom.

Colin couldn't take his eyes off Józef. For the past year, he had wanted nothing more than to return to Poland to do something to prevent his great-uncle's future death. Now, this might be their final goodbye. "Uncle Józef, Elise, and I looked up the medical diagnosis for what the doctor said might be wrong. Naomi's going to need antibiotics, and the only solution is for us to go back home. Right now."

Naomi's sleep was so sound that she didn't even hear.

A single tear fell onto Elise's cheek like a drop of dew. "We can't return to the convent. There's no time for saying goodbye to anyone but you and Anna."

"How is that going to happen?" Józef asked.

"Last time, it happened when our cell phone powered down to zero, but there was also a big explosion when the Germans were blowing up V-2 missiles near the church. To be honest, I don't know which thing triggered it. One of them."

"Or could it have been both together?" Elise asked.

"Well, we can't wait around for bombs to fall," Colin said.

"How much time do you have?" Józef asked.

"Maybe fifteen minutes. Let's bring Naomi down to the courtyard and set up the tent." Colin said.

Elise placed a cooled napkin on Naomi's brow. "Naomi, we're going to take you home to your mom and dad now."

Naomi lay in bed, with the top of her cheeks flushed by the fever, and seemed quite detached from what was happening. Elise tried to rouse Naomi by encouraging her to take a sip of tea, but was met by a resistant growl.

Although Colin knew they would soon say goodbye, he also felt a sense of regret. The three had been working as a team without argument. Everyone they met remarked they were like a miracle from God. If only they could stay longer and save more babies. "I'll go set up the tent. Elise will find all the supplies we brought."

"What about our clothes at the convent?" Elise asked.

"I guess we'll just have to surprise Mom and Dad with this Polish clothing." Colin imagined his father Greg's face when he saw him in such elegant clothing. "I really want to be back in my jersey, shorts, and comfortable shoes."

Józef smiled and appreciated how much the children had sacrificed in heroic and in many small ways. He put his arm on Colin's shoulder as the two left the room to finalize the departure.

"I thought you girls looked adorable in those sateen

dresses," Anna said. "And those bows."

"Yeah, but now our clothes sort of smell of baby pee," Elise smirked, but then thought about the possibility of returning home. "At night, I really missed my parents and everyone back home. During the day, we were always so busy that I hardly had time to remember them."

Elise studied her sweet cousin, who had been so very brave over the past month. In many ways, she had matured into almost an adult. Naomi had always seemed more resilient than other kids her age, and these events in the past weeks proved it. "Should I try harder to wake up Naomi?"

"No, she needs to sleep and heal. I have some cold tea set aside here for her to drink before we head downstairs." Tears streamed down Anna's cheeks as she grabbed Elise's hands. "I need to go tell the Countess that you are leaving."

Ten minutes later, Józef appeared at the door. "The tent is ready."

"Naomi, Uncle Józef is going to carry you downstairs," Anna whispered into Naomi's ear. Józef lifted her out of bed. Colin carried the pillows Countess Jablonowska insisted they bring into the tent to keep Naomi comfortable.

The Countess waited at the bottom of the massive staircase with the ornate leaf carvings. "I have a gift for each of you. For the girls, I have two brooches that were once my mother's. They both have these precious garnets embedded in the brooch. Garnets are said to foster passion and courage, although the girls certainly have been blessed with both."

"Oh, it's beautiful!" Elise's eyes lit up at the elegant

brooch resembling stars radiating from the larger garnets. Anna pinned it on Elise's dress.

"Oh, it's no longer there!" the Countess exclaimed. "I suppose that is a good thing since only safe people can see it."

"For Naomi, I have a similar one that has many stars. My mother used to say that a star brooch would keep a person from harm."

"It's as bright as a zinnia. Naomi will love it." Anna said.

"And for Colin, something extraordinary, the Gold Medal for Bravery. It was given to my great-great-grandfather. That's an image of Ferdinand I on the medal. He was the emperor of the Austrian Empire at that time."

Colin's eyes fluttered as Józef placed it over his head. "I don't know what to say, but I guess this is a great honor. I sure don't deserve this."

The Countess drew in a deep breath. "Colin, I want you to tell others back in America about what you have seen and the incredible sacrifices people here in Poland are making to help others. The sisters at the convent, the priests, the partisans in the forests, Józef, Anna. Many people help others at the risk of their own lives. Don't let people forget."

"We had better move quickly. I hear some thunder." Anna hesitated. "I wish I could kiss Naomi goodbye." Her quivering voice reflected everyone's sadness at the children's imminent return home. "You three have been as precious as my own family, but I look forward to seeing you again in two years."

"How can we endure two more years of the occupation?" Józef asked.

"But you will both marry nice people and have families of your own after the war. Poland will eventually be a free country." Elise wanted to be encouraging, but informing them about the forty-five years of Russian occupation after the Germans left might be too disheartening.

Józef laid Naomi on the comfortable pillows inside the tent and kissed her forehead before crawling outside. "Anna and I won't be around when you three are born in the future. Maybe you'll meet our children. That would be so nice. I hope your family remains in contact with their relatives in Poland. What would we have done these past thirty years without your great-grandfather's gifts from America?"

"Should I pack some food for the children's trip back home?" the Countess asked.

Elise giggled. "Tell her no, thank you. Hopefully, we'll be back home instantly if the cell phone works like last time."

"I'll leave your family to say the final goodbyes. I'm taking the last two babies early this evening to some good people in our parish."

The three children settled inside the tent, with Józef and Anna kneeling just outside the tent door.

"I guess it's time to start our countdown. I'll turn on the cell phone." Colin said.

"Do you want us to check anything with the cell phone? No reason to waste the battery." Elise said.

"Yes, when does Hitler die?" Józef asked. Colin punched in "Hitler's death."

"He committed suicide by gunshot on 30 April 1945 in his Führerbunker in Berlin. Eva Braun, his wife of one day, committed suicide with Hitler by taking cyanide.

Good thing I took German for the last two years. Those Germans have long words!" Colin remarked.

"We all knew Hitler was a despicable coward!" Józef yelled.

"When do the Germans leave Poland? Anna asked.

Colin's eyes skimmed the many paragraphs for that search. "It looks like they start to get pushed out by the Russians from the east and then the Allies from the other regions. The war officially ended on May 8, 1945. It was called V-E Day or Victory in Europe when General Alfred Jodl of the German high command signed the unconditional surrender of all German forces."

"We're at five percent now. We should probably say goodbye." Elise chuckled. "Unless you want to come back with us."

The look on both Anna and Józef's faces revealed they were quickly considering that offer. "What would a poor Polish guy like me do in America? No thanks." Józef momentarily struggled with the appeal of being free and not living in constant danger. Both he and Anna had made a vow to fight for Poland's freedom. Better to die for a just cause than abandon his family and fellow partisans.

"Our families wouldn't understand. They might think we had been killed or taken to a labor camp." A wave of sadness overcame Anna. "No, we need to stay here, but I'll keep dreaming of freedom like Americans have."

Lightning appeared at a distance, and the intervals of thunder indicated the storm was approaching. A huffing wind rose up, stirring the tent's flaps and whipping up the leaves in the nearby trees.

Waves of goodbyes and good wishes faded as they

began to repeat themselves. "Wait, I want to take your picture so I can show our parents." Colin aimed the cell phone camera at these two people the children had so easily grown to love.

Józef and Anna knelt outside the tent, trying to smile for the photo, but a slow chorus of raindrops pelted the tent. "Okay, now a selfie of us." Just as Elise clicked the camera, Naomi began to rouse. "What?" she said sleepily. "I don't want to leave now."

"We're going home, Naomi. There's no turning back." Colin and Elise wrapped their arms around her, holding tight as if the strength of their embrace could guarantee they would all make it back. They glanced at Józef and Anna one last time, drinking in every detail of their faces, desperate to etch this final goodbye into memory.

The cellphone screen flickered—*shutting down*—and then went black. Dead.

But the children were still in the tent. Still in Poland.

"What's going on? We're still here!" Colin's voice cracked, part disbelief, part rising panic. The phone lay useless in his palm.

A low, distant rumble rolled across the sky, deep and menacing, like something alive. Then, as if the heavens were waiting for that signal, the rain began. Sloppy, uneven drops fell at first, then they grew more insistent, drumming against the canvas.

A flash of light tore through the darkness, not a single strike, but a vast, branching web of white fire spreading across the entire sky. For a heartbeat, the world glowed ghostly white.

Then the tent shuddered violently. The central pole gave way with a loud crack, and the roof collapsed, pressing the wet canvas down over their heads. All three screamed as the storm swallowed them whole.

Chapter Twenty-Eight

Back Home

At first, it was only silence, but then a chorus of cicadas and tree frogs rang from the ravine. Their shrill, relentless whine faded, and then, seconds later, they started up their circular song.

Elise and Colin pulled the window flap to peer outside. "I think we're back in Grandma's backyard!" Colin shouted. "I'll go get Grandma and Papa. You wait here with Naomi."

Noah and Leia greeted Colin with the enthusiasm of someone who hadn't seen their loved one for ten years. Colin bolted through the door and yelled for his grandparents, who were still watching television in the family room.

Mark startled. "What in the world? Where did you get that outfit?

"You need to come outside to see Naomi. She's really sick," Colin said.

Donna put on her robe and slippers. "She was just fine an hour ago."

There was no reason to hide the truth, as both his grandparents knew of their last adventure. "We were in Poland again. During the war. Naomi probably got bit by fleas or something, or got sick from the babies. Elise and I brought her home right away to get her medical help.

The doctor in Poland couldn't help."

Mark bolted out the back door, carried Naomi inside, and put her on the couch. "Colin, you call your parents and tell your dad to get right over here with his medical bag."

Donna held the thermometer in Naomi's mouth. "She may just have some kind of infection, like an ear infection."

"Grandma, the doctor in Poland said it might be typhus or scarlet fever. They didn't have any antibiotics or medicines, so we decided to end our adventure."

"So, you guys lit the gromnica again? Even after your parents had forbidden it?"

"It was Naomi, but don't make her feel bad. It was all worth it." Colin said.

"Oh, honey, please don't ever do this again. How many days were you in Poland?

"Two or three weeks. Maybe a month. We helped Monsignor Dunajecki and nuns at the convent save Jewish babies and children."

Donna's eyes then fell upon the brooch on Elise's dress. "What in the world? Let me see that jewelry. It couldn't have come from the poor nuns or my family."

"Countess Jablonowska gave them to us for bravery. Anna said these brooches are probably worth a lot of money. She gave Colin an old medal for bravery."

When they arrived at the front door, Jessica and Greg took only a few seconds to know what had happened. "I thought we made it clear that lighting the gromnica was strictly forbidden," Jessica said.

Elise hugged her mother. "It was Naomi, but now she's really sick. We came home so she wouldn't die."

Greg checked her temperature and did a brief

inspection. "If it's typhus, Doxycycline would be what any doctor would prescribe."

"Greg, if you call in a prescription, I'll find a drugstore that's still open," Mark said.

Chapter Twenty-Nine

Should We Return?

Two days later, Elise and Colin arrived at their grandparents' house to visit the recovering Naomi. The first night was a restless one, worrying about their young cousin's recovery. They had spent the past day telling their parents about their adventures.

Naomi's grandparents called her parents Brittany and Culdry that first evening. They drove from their home in North Carolina as soon as they heard what had happened.

"Hi, Aunt Brittany! We came to see how Naomi is doing. Is she still upstairs in bed?" Elise asked.

"She's doing great. No temperature this morning, and she ate a bit for breakfast," Brittany said. "You guys have to tell me your version of the adventure in Poland. It sounds like you packed a lifetime of adventure into a few weeks!"

"After we check on Naomi, we'll show you what the countess gave us! We have a few pictures on our cellphones, too!" Colin said. "Naomi is one brave kid!"

"She's in the family room, watching her favorite shows," Culdry said.

Elise ran up to her cousin, who was relaxing in the recliner, watching television.

"You're looking like the old Naomi we all love,"

Elise said. "How are you feeling?"

"Better than I felt yesterday. Hey, do you guys have my cell phone?

"Yep, and we charged it all up. Wait until your parents see our pictures." Colin said. "Look, here's a picture of us finding a home for a Jewish baby. Here's a photo of Countess Helena. Here's one of Józef and Anna saying goodbye."

"What about Father Kurek?" Naomi asked.

"Oh, sorry. We didn't get any of Sister Roberta or Sister Aniela either." Elise said. I wish we could go back and do a better job of getting proof that we were really there."

Brittany gave her much-used teacher look to the children. "You aren't even thinking of going back again. Are you?"

Greg hovered over Naomi and then finished up a brief exam. "I'd say Naomi is really on the mend. I'll do a blood draw again and send it to the lab."

Brittany sat on the floor next to Naomi's recliner. "So, Greg. Do you have the test results back yet?"

"It looks pretty conclusive that it was typhus." Greg put his stethoscope back in his medical bag. Colin and Elise did the right thing by getting Naomi back home for an antibiotic. I doubt she would have died from it because her health was so good going into this. The same can't be said for the people who lived in such poor conditions and near starvation during the war. Typhus would have been a death sentence for them."

"I promise that I won't try to go back, but if you were there, you guys would have seen how helpful we were getting the Jewish babies out of danger. We could do things no one else could because we were invisible."

Elise said.

Colin nodded. "This time was a lot scarier, believe it or not. We came across several bad people who could see us. One of them was Sister Aniela's disgusting brother named Mishka. I managed to snap a picture of him when we met him the second time."

Elise brought the cell phone so Brittany and Culdry could see Mishka's blurry photo. "Wow, he's a really grubby-looking character," Brittany said. "Did that guy Mishka scare you, Naomi?"

Naomi sat up in the recliner, who by now had her old spunk back. "Are you kidding, Mom? I wasn't afraid of Mishka. Anyway, he got knocked off by the Home Army."

Colin burst out laughing. "Wow, Naomi. You're pretty war-hardened. Where did you get the idea that the Home Army knocked him off?"

"I think she means the partisans killed him because he was the cause of so many people's deaths. And that's not how I remember Mishka. Everyone was scared of Mishka, even the grown-ups." Elise said.

Donna walked over to her treasured gromnica and took it off its honored place on the mantle. "First, my two oldest grandchildren traveled to WWII and became Home Army partisans. Then all of my grandkids find themselves in the middle of the Holocaust, rescuing Jewish babies."

Donna turned around to look at her three precious adventurers. "Are you hoping to go back again? Tell me the truth."

The three shrugged and sat still with their eyes staring at the carpet.

"Seeing Naomi so sick made me wonder if going

back was the right thing to do," Elise said. "I think I've had enough adventure." Then, under her breath, she muttered, "For now."

"But I'm okay now. Next time, we'll prepare ourselves and bring antibiotics." Naomi said.

"Naomi, antibiotics may not be what you would need next time. I think you three have had enough adventure for a lifetime," her grandfather said.

"Not for a while. I promise," Colin said. "But, when I'm older. I need to get back before Uncle Józef commits suicide."

"Colin, you can't predict what year you'll be sent to. Maybe the gromnica will send you to Poland when my grandparents lived there." Donna said.

"That would be so cool!" Naomi scrunched her face while she pondered that possibility. "Then our answer is yes! We're going back someday!"

Colin looked at the old medal that had been gifted to him by the Countess. "Grandma, Papa. I don't think it was the gromnica sending us back. It was God. He wanted us to help the partisans and help the Allies learn about the V-2 to help the war effort. Just like God put bravery in all people's hearts this last time, God is the one who sent us there."

Everyone sat silently, and then Elise ran to Colin's side and hugged him. Naomi quickly joined her cousins with her blanket in tow.

Donna carefully wrapped the gromnica in a protective cloth. "Oh, Colin. We know you are right, but this gromnica is going under lock and key for a while."

"Can we see it again before you put it away?" Elise asked.

"Nobody has a match or lighter? Right?" Donna

handed over the gromnica to Elise.

The children examined the lovely golden gromnica. "It sure is pretty with the carved wax flowers,' said Elise.

Colin lifted his cell phone, his hands trembling with urgency. The gromnica's delicate wax carvings and intricate designs glowed softly in the dim light. It might be years before they ever laid eyes on it again. He pressed the camera button. A faint *click* echoed unnaturally loud in the stillness of the room.

Then it happened.

As if the captured image had unleashed something ancient and unseen, the air shuddered. A sudden, invisible force rippled outward, rattling the windows and making the very floorboards quiver beneath their feet.

The adults whipped their heads toward the children. Their eyes widened in horror, each frozen for a breathless heartbeat as the scene unraveled before them.

And in the next blink—Colin, Elise, and Naomi were gone.

The room fell into an eerie silence. Only the gromnica remained, resting harmlessly on the sofa, its unblemished wax gleaming as though nothing had happened… and yet everything had.

A word about the author...

Donna Gawell is an accomplished genealogist, historian, and author of numerous published books and journal articles. Her passion for history and family heritage shines through in her historical novels and most recent book, Our Galician Ancestors.

Donna and her husband, Mark, enjoy traveling to Europe for research and meeting local historians and residents to uncover the previously unknown stories of courage and bravery. She is also a presenter on genealogy, travel, history, and family history writing for community and history organizations. Donna holds volunteer leadership roles with Samaritan's Purse and LifeWise Academy.

Donna earned a master's degree in Speech Pathology and worked in education for over thirty-five years. Her website, DonnaGawell.com, allows her to reach out to readers with similar passions and interests.

DonnaGawell.com

www.ingramcontent.com/pod-product-compliance
Lightning Source LLC
Chambersburg PA
CBHW070517260626
47161CB00004B/1575